Shoot-Out

Shoot-Out

a Comeback Kids novel

MIKE LUPICA

PHILOMEL BOOKS /  **WALDEN MEDIA**

PHILOMEL BOOKS

A division of Penguin Young Readers Group.

Published by The Penguin Group.

Penguin Group (USA) Inc., 375 Hudson Street, New York, NY 10014, U.S.A.
Penguin Group (Canada), 90 Eglinton Avenue East, Suite 700, Toronto, Ontario M4P
2Y3, Canada (a division of Pearson Penguin Canada Inc.). Penguin Books Ltd, 80
Strand, London WC2R 0RL, England. Penguin Ireland, 25 St. Stephen's Green, Dublin
2, Ireland (a division of Penguin Books Ltd). Penguin Group (Australia), 250 Camber-
well Road, Camberwell, Victoria 3124, Australia (a division of Pearson Australia Group
Pty Ltd). Penguin Books India Pvt Ltd, 11 Community Centre, Panchsheel Park, New
Delhi - 110 017, India. Penguin Group (NZ), 67 Apollo Drive, Rosedale, North Shore
0632, New Zealand (a division of Pearson New Zealand Ltd). Penguin Books (South
Africa) (Pty) Ltd, 24 Sturdee Avenue, Rosebank, Johannesburg 2196, South Africa.
Penguin Books Ltd, Registered Offices: 80 Strand, London WC2R 0RL, England.

This book is published in partnership with Walden Media, LLC. Walden Media and the
Walden Media skipping stone logo are trademarks and registered trademarks of Walden
Media, LLC, 294 Washington Street, Boston, MA 02108.

Published simultaneously in Canada.

Printed in the United States of America.

Text set in Bookman.

Library of Congress Cataloging-in-Publication Data
Lupica, Mike. Shoot-out : a Comeback Kids novel / Mike Lupica. p. cm. Summary:
Twelve-year-old Jake must leave his championship soccer team to play on a team with
a losing record when his family moves to a neighboring town. [1. Soccer—Fiction.
2. Winning and losing—Fiction. 3. Moving, Household—Fiction.] I. Title. PZ7.L97914
Sho 2009 [Fic]—dc22 2008021588
ISBN 978-0-399-24718-7

3 5 7 9 10 8 6 4 2

For Chris, Alex, Zach and Hannah. You all made me as happy watching you play soccer as you did everywhere else. And for the former Taylor McKelvy, of course.

ACKNOWLEDGMENTS

Andrea Montalbano, a fine writer in her own right, who was so generous with her wisdom and her soccer expertise.

For Coach Henk Hartong, who made me appreciate the finer points of the game in all the seasons we coached our daughters.

And for Richard Williams, head coach at St. Luke's, who coached two of my sons and shared his passion for the game. And who gave Zach Lupica a season he will remember for the rest of his life.

ONE

Jake Stuart was the man now.

Oh yeah, *definitely* the man, playing the only position he ever wanted to play, center mid, feeling like the center of everything now, the whole game going through him.

Breaking into the clear at midfield, plenty of green in front of him, dribbling the ball like a total pro, like one of his heroes, the ball on a string with both feet, Jake feeling the way he always did in moments like these, as if the field were tilting away from him.

As if he were running downhill.

Jake thought: *Please let everybody stay onside. Wingers, strikers, everybody.*

Please just wait for me this one time.

No whistles.

That was all the help he was going to need. He'd already made up his mind that somehow, whatever it took, he was going to figure out a way to take it all the way, that he was going to score himself this time.

He just hadn't let anybody else in on his little secret, at least not yet.

Jake totally loved this part, running in the open field even before he got into the box, before things got a lot more crowded, like somebody had shrunk the huge field to something that felt like the inside of a school bus. Jake loved the moment—a moment at full speed—when you started to make something happen, when you turned defense into offense all by yourself.

Coach Lord called Jake his "coach on the field."

All game long, the center mid for Lincoln's twelve-year-old travel team had been coming up hard on Jake when he'd try to make any kind of play. The other kid had figured out early that if he could be aggressive with Jake, knock him off the ball first chance he got, before Jake got a head of steam going for him, that Jake's team—Belmont—

had hardly any chance of pushing the ball, forcing the action, in any kind of serious way.

Smart kid.

One who knew that if he could force Jake to pass before he wanted to, Lincoln's outside guys could shut down the play every single time, pick Jake's teammates clean.

And just like that, Jake would be back on defense, throwing his own game into reverse, knowing he had to help out the guys behind him. Even with all the help he was supposed to have behind him on defense, stoppers and sweepers and fullbacks set up like a defensive backfield in football, Jake still felt a little bit like it was him against the world.

But Lincoln's center mid hung back this time.

Maybe it was because he was just gassed by now. Maybe he was being lazy, assuming this would be another time when Jake was going to give the ball up early, even this late in the game.

Whatever.

Didn't matter.

Jake had room to maneuver now.

Like finally having room to breathe.

The big scoreboard at Belmont Middle School

was behind him, on the parking lot end of the field, but Jake knew there had been thirty seconds left when he started up the field.

Plenty of time, he told himself. His ball now. For the last seconds of this game, *his* game.

At last.

Quinn O'Dell, Jake's best friend on the team, Belmont's goalie, always said that Jake didn't just have eyes in back of his head, he had them on both sides of his head, too. Sometimes Jake really felt as if he did. It was why he knew, just *knew* as he slowed down a little, that his guys weren't offsides, that they hadn't gone too far ahead of the play and behind the last Lincoln defender. Cal Morris was running a step behind over on his right, and his left middie, Matt Purcell, was farther behind than that to Jake's left. He knew that because Matt was the one who'd been acting gassed the whole second half.

Jake knew all that the way he knew what was going to happen at the end of this play. What was going to happen was that he was going to put the ball behind the Lincoln goalie. Control things right until the ball was behind that hot dog.

Finally—*finally*—this was the way it was supposed to be, the way things were supposed to work out for him in the last minute of a game.

Jake saw it all: Their center mid laying back, the outside guys inching up anyway, as if Jake were going to pass it to Cal or Matt just by force of habit. Give it up for the team one more time.

Only sometimes, especially this close to the end, the best way to be a team guy was to score the goal.

Seemed like a plan.

Jake moved the ball to his left foot, which usually meant a pass to Cal on the right. The Lincoln kid, a tall redhead, face full of freckles, forgot about making the sliding-tackle move he'd been making on Jake the whole game, and flashed to his left thinking he could pick the pass off himself.

Only Jake kept the ball on his left foot, moved into that extra gear he had, that he'd *always* had, and went flying past the redhead. He saw him slip and fall out of the corner of his eye.

Jake against their sweeper now.

Their free safety. The gambler on the Lincoln team. This guy wasn't laying back, wasn't hesitating.

He was coming right at Jake. But Jake put one of his favorite moves on him, nearly coming to a stop even though he'd been going at full speed, and put the ball behind him as he did, just for an instant. Reached back with his left leg like he was using it to shut a door behind him, like he was making a be-hind-the-back pass to himself, and just absolutely dusted the guy as he went right.

Money.

Just Jake and the goalie now.

This was the goalie who'd been talking nonstop since the game began. Talking to his teammates, to the refs, to the Belmont players, to his coach, even to his buddies in the stands. One of those guys. Com-ing way up into the field even when he didn't have to, showing off constantly, making flashier plays than he needed to make—how much did Jake hate that?—making hey-look-at-me saves and heaves and kicks and dives.

Another one on the Lincoln team who wasn't going to hang back. Wasn't his style. And this guy was *all* style. He wasn't going to be looking for his defense to bail him out, somehow get back into the play, somehow get between him and Jake.

You could see by the look on his face that this was the way he wanted it, the way it was, the way Jake wanted it:

Me against you.

Jake knew that eventually, even in team sports, it always came down to that in the end. He had always been a team man in soccer, from the beginning, but in sports you always looked for the moment when it was man-on-man, one-on-one, your best against his.

From the time Jake first started watching sports on television, he'd heard football announcers talking about how quarterbacks didn't really make it in the NFL until the game slowed down for them, until they could sit back there in the pocket and feel as if the play developing in front of them were in slow motion.

Jake felt that way now, even though he was flying, even though he'd made guys on the other team go flying past him.

Pick your spot, his mom had always told him, from the first time they were kicking the ball around in the backyard and the goal was the area between two stakes in the fence around the swimming pool.

Pick your spot unless the goalie commits first.

Most of all, don't rush.

Jake wasn't rushing.

Had to be around ten seconds left now.

Still time for him to beat this guy once and for all.

End the day right against this goalie, with his shirt that had more colors than Baskin-Robbins had flavors, with his bright red gloves and even his baseball cap turned around in a hot dog way.

The goalie clapped those red gloves now, eyeballing Jake the whole time, as if to say *bring it*.

In the words of Quinn O'Dell, who had a language all his own, the goalie was thuggin' on Jake to the end.

Jake didn't care.

Upper right corner.

That's where he was going with the shot.

But the goalie, no dope, was thinking right along with him, leaning that way.

Cake, Jake thought.

The kid had committed just enough, made up Jake's mind for him.

He could feel pressure coming now, feel the

crowd that should have been there earlier coming from behind and from the sides. But no way they were getting there in time. Jake planted his left foot, gave the ball one last small push to the outside, like he was teeing the sucker up.

Then he let it go.

For one shaky moment he thought he'd leaned back and got too far under it, that it might go sailing over the crossbar. And how many times had Jake seen that happen, a shooter alone in the box, all set up, getting too amped up and sending it deep into the woods?

Not this time.

The best part, the very best part, was that the Lincoln goalie was *so* sure of himself to the end. He was going to dazzle everybody with one more save, launch himself one last time like he was auditioning to get himself into SportsCenter's Top 10 Plays.

He had cheated a step to his left, shifting his weight, ready to pounce.

But Jake had put one last fake on the guy. The goalie went one way as the ball went the other. It wasn't just the ball Jake had on a string now; it was like he'd turned the goalie into a puppet that he'd flung to the side.

The ball tucked itself into the top corner, the strings of the net making Jake feel as if he'd swished one in hoops, as neatly as a hand fitting into a glove.

Goal.

But Jake didn't celebrate, didn't run around the way guys in other sports did at times like this, as if they've forgotten what the scoreboard said.

Jake hadn't forgotten.

Jake turned and took one last look at that scoreboard now, just because he couldn't make himself look anywhere else from where he stood on the field.

Visitors 6, Belmont 1.

It felt like the longest game of Jake's life.

And it was only the first game of the season.

TWO

Jake didn't hate his new town.

He actually liked the town of Belmont and liked their new house, mostly because his new room was twice the size of his old one. He loved that his dad had finally agreed to buy a ginormous television for the basement, to go along with the new pool table.

And he liked Belmont Middle School. It had taken about five minutes of his first bus ride on the first day of school for him and Quinn O'Dell to become buds—Quinn said they were "boys"—before he even found out Quinn lived at the end of his street. By the time the first week of school was over, it was as if he and Quinn had been best friends their whole lives.

No, it wasn't Belmont that Jake disliked. It was their so-bad-it-actually-hurt twelve-year-old travel soccer team.

Cal and Matt were the two best forwards on the team, but that wasn't saying very much. Jake liked them, too. And Doug Warner, the stopper, definitely the second-best player on the team after Jake, was probably the funniest kid in their grade.

Jake liked them all. And they all tried really hard.

Didn't change the fact that the team was terrible.

Jake, who had played on the best eleven-year-old team in the whole state last year when he was still living in Greenville, a much bigger town about fifteen miles away, knew they were in trouble the first day of tryouts, and nothing that had happened since had changed his mind.

The "Boys 12" team from Belmont was going to be the flat-out, hands-down, guaranteed worst in the Madison County Premier League. Or, as Jake was already thinking of it, the Madison County Premier League plus Belmont.

Jake really couldn't see them winning a single game, considering what he'd seen in the league last year. Greenville had played Belmont twice in the 11's.

First game: 6–2.

Second game: 5–0.

He had been sure today's score was going to be something similar, especially after Lincoln was leading 4–0 at the half. But when they built the lead up to 6–0 two minutes into the second half, Jake could see their coach, who had moved up with these kids from the 11's, tell them to stop trying to score.

It happened during a break in the action, when Cal rolled an ankle and Coach Lord ran out on the field along with the trainer to see how bad it was. The Lincoln coach took that opportunity to call his guys over, and Jake saw him raising his fist in the air, signaling for them to play two-touch. The soccer version of keep-away.

He told them that if they did put a ball on the goal, it had better be from long range.

Jake thought: It's kinda like the soccer version, the *travel* soccer version, of the mercy rule in Little League baseball. What kids always called the slaughter rule. If you got behind by nine runs or more and it was still early enough, they just stopped the game.

Like a boxer's trainer throwing a towel into the ring when his guy was getting beaten up too badly.

It had been that way today. The only problem—for Jake—was that he had to keep playing, even knowing the other team wasn't trying its hardest.

It was as humiliating as anything, more humiliating in Jake's mind than even the final score would be.

The only reason he knew the Lincoln kids were still trying on defense in the last minute was because he could see how much they wanted to preserve the shutout for their hot dog goalie.

The best hot dog in Belmont, Jake knew, was at a place called Mango King in the Belmont Mall. As the game wore on, that was how he started thinking of the Lincoln goalie:

The Mango King.

Jake could see in the last few minutes how much he wanted to stick it to Belmont one last time by shutting them out, and he could see it by the way Lincoln's stopper and sweeper and their outside guys on defense were still grinding. That's why Jake knew he had *really* scored, that his rush through those guys had been totally legit. Because this team was legit, as good as Greenville had been last year in the 11's.

"From first to worst," the Mango King had said to Jake early in the game. "Dude, that must be, like, *so* gnarly."

Jake didn't say anything. It wasn't written down in any rulebook, but when you were getting beaten the way his team was today, you just had to shut up and take it—no matter how much trash the other guys talked.

And how mad could he get, anyway? He *had* gone from first to worst. Greenville had been un-beaten in the 11's and was probably going to be unbeaten in the 12's, with all of Jake's former team-mates back.

Except Jake, of course.

Who'd moved three towns over.

The move had been no big shock. Jake's dad had been talking about doing it for a couple of years, wanting to stop commuting to his law firm in the city and open a practice of his own. Last spring he'd announced he was finally doing it, that he'd found exactly the right spot in Belmont and that Jake's mom had found the "perfect house."

As soon as the school year had ended, they'd moved.

"But all my friends are on the soccer team," Jake had said.

His dad had smiled and said, "There are always good reasons not to do something like this. Unfortunately, bud, travel soccer isn't one of them."

"I feel like I'm getting traded," Jake had said.

"I prefer to think of it as a highly sought-after free agent playing out his option and switching teams," his dad had said.

Jake remembered his father's words now and wanted to tell him that even if they had given him free-agent money, he wouldn't have wanted to switch to *this* team.

When the guys finished their snacks, Coach John Lord called them over and told them to get in a circle. When they were all there, Coach reminded them that it was only one game, that everybody knew Lincoln was going to be one of the stud teams in the Madison County League, that he didn't want to see anybody hanging their head because Lincoln had done to them what they were going to do to a lot of teams this season.

"I've never had a team that didn't get better as the season went along," he said. "I told you something the first day we were together as a team, and I'm going to tell you the same thing now: I don't measure this thing in W's and L's alone. I measure it on how much every single guy on this team improves from the start of the season till the end."

Jake knew he was a good coach, one he could see was really into soccer, who could talk to Jake about Beckham and Platini and Zidane the head-butter. One who really did want guys on the team to improve.

Despite that, all Jake was really hearing now was this:

Blah blah blah.

He just wanted this day to be over. Coach could talk all day, talk until it started to get dark, but 6–1 wasn't going to change.

When Coach Lord was through, Jake walked back over to where his parents were waiting for him.

His dad said, "Can I at least tell you that really was a great play at the end?"

Jake smiled, trying to make a joke of it. "I don't want your pity."

His mom said, "It *was* a great play, honey. And you know it."

His mom had been a soccer star in college at the University of North Carolina. She had been a center middie, too, and she had been the one who taught Jake, from the time she first started teaching him the game, that a good center mid did more to control the flow of the game than anybody else on the field.

So he had been a center mid from the time he was still playing seven to a side, when the boys were still playing on the same team with girls and when Saturday morning soccer could look like ants trying to move a piece of food just by kicking it. It was why Jake's heroes were guys who were playmakers: Pelé, and Zidane, the French guy who went nuts and head-butted a guy in the World Cup final back in 2006. Even an Italian player he'd learned about on YouTube, Baggio, who'd missed the last penalty kick in another World Cup final one time.

But the truth was, his first soccer hero had been his mom, who was now saying to him, "And you *re-*

ally know that it just killed that big-mouth keeper to lose his shutout that close to the end of the game."

Never a *goalie* with his mom. Always a *keeper.* When it came to soccer, Grace Stuart always talked the talk.

"He *was* annoying," Jake said.

"I hope we play him again," his mom said.

It was the jock in her coming out. Jake would see it sometimes when they were goofing around in the backyard, where she'd set up a regulation goal. If she decided Jake wasn't going to get around her, he wasn't.

"*You* may want to see him again," Jake said. "But I don't."

His dad got up and put his arm around him and said, "I know you're scuffling right now. But things will get better, I promise."

"Don't make a promise I can't deliver, Dad." He turned to his mom and said, "Were you ever on a team that stunk?"

"Sure," she said.

"Truth?"

"Junior year in high school," she said. "We were three-and-seventeen."

"What was that like?" Jake said.

"I'll tell you what it was like," she said. "I was as proud of those three wins as could be. Because we might not have won a game at all if I hadn't sucked it up. Which is what you're going to have to do."

"Lucky me," Jake said.

Quinn O'Dell came running over then. Jake's dad called him "The Mighty Quinn," which he said was a name that came from some old song. The Mighty Quinn who never got down about anything—not even having six balls end up in the net behind him.

"My mom said it's okay if you come over," Quinn said.

He was out of breath, but Quinn seemed to go through life out of breath, as if he just kept running from one adventure to the next.

"Oh, hello Mr. and Mrs. Stuart," he said, as if he'd just noticed them standing there.

"I know no one who just saw the score would understand this," Jake's dad said, "but you were great today, Quinn."

Jake's mom said, "If it hadn't been for you, I

don't even want to think about what the final score would have been."

Quinn grinned at them. His face was still dirty from the game, and the front of his goalie shirt looked as if it had no chance of being clean ever again.

"I'm afraid to turn around, Mrs. S. If I do, their striker's probably scoring on me again."

Quinn turned to Jake then and said, "You ready to bounce?"

"Only if you promise we don't have to talk about the game for the rest of the day," Jake said.

"What game?" Quinn said.

They started toward the parking lot. As they walked, they noticed Kevin Crosby still sitting at the end of their bench, the same spot where he'd spent most of the game after telling Coach Lord he wasn't feeling well.

They both watched now as Kevin slowly unlaced his spikes, took them off, stood up so he could slip on his warm-up pants, sat back down, and switched into his sneakers.

It was as if he had all day, nowhere to go.

His dad stood next to him, waiting.

Jake wanted to go over there and say something

to him, had been wanting to say something since Kevin had come back to school about a week ago, and finally rejoined the team at practice the previous Wednesday night.

But Jake didn't know what to say.

He stood there feeling as overwhelmed at the idea of trying to find the right words as he had felt playing Lincoln.

All he knew is what the other kids in school knew, what the other guys on the team knew, that Kevin's mom—whom Jake had never met—had died after being sick a long time.

Jake felt a hand on his shoulder then.

Quinn's.

"You know what?" Quinn said in a quiet voice from behind him. "Maybe getting boxed around in a soccer game isn't the worst thing in the world."

THREE

Kevin Crosby took the same bus to Belmont Middle that Jake and Quinn did.

He got on two stops before them, and every morning it was the same. Jake and Quinn would get on at the corner of East River Road, and Kevin would be in a seat five or six rows from the back. The seat next to him would always be empty, and there Kevin would be, staring out the window, not talking to anybody the whole way to school.

This Monday was no different. When Jake and Quinn got on the bus, Kevin was in his usual spot.

In a low voice Jake said, "What was he like before his mom got sick?"

"He's always been quiet," Quinn said, "just not like he is now. But a pretty cool guy. We usually played on the same soccer team and the same baseball team."

"You guys hung out?"

"Not that much," Quinn said. "He was best buds with this kid, Dave Wirth, but Dave's dad got transferred to London and they moved in August, right before school started."

"Whoa," Jake said. "He lost his best friend *and* his mom?"

"Stinks, right?"

"Royally."

Jake turned back around so he wasn't staring at Kevin. "No wonder he's so sad-looking all the time," he said. "I would be, too."

At the next stop, Dustin Sawyer's mom came sprinting out of their front door in her bathrobe, came right up the bus stairs and asked the driver to please wait, Dustin couldn't find his sneakers.

There were a lot of mornings when Dustin's mom came out frantic because Dustin had forgotten something and she didn't want to end up driving him to school.

"The way Dustin smells sometimes," Quinn said, "I'm thinking that maybe his sneakers didn't want to find *him*."

It was then that Jake decided to go sit with Kevin Crosby, say something about his mom before he lost his nerve. He walked down the aisle, managed not to trip when Matt Purcell stuck his leg out, and said to Kevin, "This seat taken?"

Kevin gave a little shake of his head, almost like Jake had awakened him. "Huh?"

Jake nodded at the seat. "You mind?"

It wasn't like Kevin could say he was saving it for somebody, since the seat was always empty on the way to school and going home. So Kevin grabbed his backpack, dropped it on the floor in front him, and said, "Suit yourself."

Jake and Kevin both watched out the window now as Dustin came tearing down his front walk, nearly tripped on his shoelaces as he came up the steps to the bus, and immediately started apologizing to everybody for keeping them waiting.

All he got was loudly trash-talked in return.

"Whoa," Cal Morris called out from the back. "This bus smells like feet all of a sudden."

Then Matt Purcell said, "Dude, that is like *so* insulting to feet."

"Wait a second," Cal said, pointing at Dustin's sneakers. "I thought I killed those kicks on Halo last night."

While that was going on, Jake said to Kevin, "Kev, I've been meaning to tell you, I'm real sorry about your mom."

Jake was sure he saw Kevin's shoulders sag.

"Thanks."

Still looking out the window.

"I don't know what else to say," Jake said.

"Don't worry," Kevin said. "That's pretty much what everybody says."

The bus, which always sounded to Jake like a garbage disposal when the driver was putting it into gear, was in motion again, two stops left before Belmont Middle.

Jake felt like the one trying to get into gear with Kevin Crosby. "I mean, if there's anything I can do, or anything you need . . ."

Kevin turned. Jake saw that his eyes were red. Not crying red, but close enough.

"There's not," he said.

Jake had only come back here because he was trying to be a good guy, because he felt like he'd waited too long to say something to Kevin. Because he felt like you were supposed to be a good teammate even when what you were doing had nothing to do with the team.

Only now that Jake was sitting here next to him, having the conversation with him he'd been putting off—if you could call it a conversation—it occurred to him that he didn't know Kevin at all.

As a classmate or a teammate.

And he sure didn't know anybody who'd ever had happen to them what had happened to Kevin.

"You don't have to do this," Kevin said in a quiet voice.

"I didn't come back here because I felt like I had to," Jake said.

"Yeah," Kevin said, "you did."

Kevin sat up a little and turned to the window, almost like he was turning his back on Jake. It was why Jake was barely able to hear what he said next, even though it was one of those times on the bus when everybody seemed to stop talking at once.

"I just want everybody to leave me alone," he said.

FOUR

Jake had seen guys who didn't care about sports, even though they played them. Had seen them on every team he'd ever played for, soccer or basketball or baseball.

There were guys who didn't care because they weren't good enough and knew they were never going to be good enough, so they ended up making a joke out of the whole thing, acted like they didn't want to be there, when all they really wanted to be was better.

Then there were guys who didn't care because they just didn't love sports, not the way Jake did. Or the way Quinn did. Especially Quinn. When it came to soccer this season, he was going to have to take it more than anybody else on the team. He was going to be the duck in the shooting gallery, game after game after game.

Quinn didn't care. As long as he was a part of a team, as long as he was competing, he was happy. Like, Hall of Fame happy. He cared about winning as much as Jake did; Jake knew that about him. But losing—even the prospect of losing—didn't bring him down the way it brought down Jake.

No matter what the score was, Quinn O'Dell was going to defend his goal, on every shot, as if he were trying to stop a penalty kick in a tie game.

Kevin Crosby was different. Jake just figured it was because of his mom. Kevin had talent, a lot of talent. Jake would see just how much from time to time in practice, when it would just come out of Kevin, as if he'd forgotten for the moment that he didn't want to be on the field or on this team.

Kevin would make a shot or a pass or a stop that let you know there was a soccer player in-side him after all, like some genie trapped inside a bottle.

Only in his case the genie didn't want to get out.

Sometimes when they were short players, Coach

Lord would throw some of his orange cones on the field and announce that they were "ghost" players for one side or the other, and you weren't allowed to pass the ball into that particular area.

Kevin was like a ghost player.

It was the end of practice and Coach Lord was putting them through a three-on-three drill.

It happened to be one of Jake's favorites. They only used a third of the field, and one goalie for both sides: Quinn. The object of the drill was to make good, sure passes, not risk a turnover by taking the first good shot you got. If you scored, you kept the ball, same as if they were playing winners-out in a game of half-court basketball.

If Quinn made the save, the ball came back out and the other team got it.

The best part of three-on-three, at least to Jake, was that you didn't have all day, you couldn't take the air out of the ball for even ten seconds, because Coach had you on the clock: You had only thirty seconds to get off a shot.

Jake loved this game no matter how tired he'd get, no matter how many times the other guys did everything short of begging Coach to blow his whistle and rotate in new players. Jake loved having to make quick decisions with his head and with his feet, loved being able to thread the needle with a pass in a crowded area, loved finding the angle on Quinn—even though Quinn already seemed to know most of Jake's favorite angles by heart.

Now Coach announced that the next goal would win, and Jake wasn't sure why—maybe it was because he still felt so badly about the conversation he'd had with Kevin on the bus—but he was determined that Kevin would be the one to score it.

Maybe just to see if that could get a smile out of him, putting one behind Quinn.

Mike Clark, their regular sweeper, was on the other team, and so were the two other guys who were the best defenders on the team, Reid McDonough and Doug Warner.

As soon as Jake made a move and began to close on Quinn, Mike was on him, trying to smother him. Doug came from Jake's right and double-teamed him, probably figuring he didn't have to worry about Kevin, who hadn't bothered to take a single shot yet.

Jake decided it was time for his version of the Maradona Spin.

Diego Maradona didn't invent the move and wasn't the only one who used it. All of Jake's favorite guys did. But it was Maradona who'd made it famous, who seemed to use it at least once in every one of Jake's favorite videos.

Other guys on the team tried it sometimes. But Jake was the only one who could actually do it, even when he was running at top speed the way he was now.

He slowed down just enough, almost to a complete stop, but not quite. Then he did something with his right foot—what they called the "master" foot in soccer—that was known as the drag-back move: put his right instep on the ball and spun it backward.

As he did, *he* spun, to his left, and in the same motion used his left foot to drag the ball back again. Now, instead of moving straight at the goal he was moving to his right, looking for all the world like he was going to turn the corner on both Mike and Doug, because he had a step on both of them now.

And if he'd wanted to, Jake could have planted his left foot and rocketed a sidewinder shot on Quinn from where he was.

Only that's not what Jake wanted. The double-team had left Kevin wide-open.

Jake wound up like he was going to shoot. Then he eased up and passed the ball to Kevin instead. A sweet pass if there ever was one.

Or would have been a sweet pass, if Kevin had kept running.

He didn't. He'd stopped. And instead of him being on the doorstep with a shot he couldn't miss, instead of the ball meeting up with his foot, it went past him and out of bounds.

Jake couldn't help himself. He slapped his side with his hand and yelled out, "Come *on,* dude. Move your feet!"

In that moment, his voice was the only one you could hear on the field. In fact, Jake felt like it might be the only sound you could hear for *blocks,* at least until Coach Lord blew his whistle and told every-body to leave the field. He'd changed his mind—everybody was going to run tonight.

They jogged over to the place on the sidelines

where they'd tossed their bottles of water and Gatorade and Vitaminwater.

Except Jake.

"Jake, can I have a word with you?"

Coach.

Great, Jake thought. *Way to go.*

You make the perfect pass and now you're the one who's going to get chewed out.

Before Coach could say anything, Jake said, "I know I was out of line. I shouldn't have called out Kevin that way." Talking fast. "I know you're never supposed to show up a teammate."

Coach said, "No."

Jake kept going. "I mean, I thought I made a *kickin'* pass, but when I saw the ball go out I forgot who I was passing it *to.* I should've kept my dumb mouth shut. I won't do it again, I promise."

"Oh, yes you will."

Usually Jake got everything Coach Lord was saying, as if they were having a conversation about soccer that only the two of them could understand.

Not now.

"I don't understand," Jake said.

"Let me explain it to you," Coach said. "You

made the right play and you don't have to apologize because somebody didn't make it with you. You had a right to be ticked off."

"But it's Kevin," Jake said. "And I thought . . . well, I thought the rules were different when it came to Kevin."

Coach Lord sat down in the grass and motioned for Jake to sit down next to him. Jake looked over and noticed Kevin sitting alone at the end of the bench the way he had been at the end of Saturday's game.

The way he always sat alone at the back of the bus.

"We have to stop treating him this way or he's never gonna be a part of this team," Coach said. "I've been thinking about this a lot and now I'm thinking about it out loud with you. You're my star player and my coach on the field, after all."

Jake waited.

"You see what I'm saying?" Coach said. "Treat him like he's different and that's all he'll ever be. Different."

"But he *is* different," Jake said. "At least for now. And who knows? Maybe forever."

"His dad says it's important that he stays on the team," Coach said. "So from now on, he's *going* to be on it. Even if it means we get on his butt once in a while when he messes up."

"We?" Jake said.

"I need your help on this, Jake. The other kids on the team don't just look to you for what you bring to the game, they look up to you *because* of it. So I need you to push him the way I see you trying to push the other guys."

"Coach . . ."

"Let me finish," Coach said, looking up to the sky now as if the right words were floating around up there. "Somehow we've got to find a way to bring this boy back."

Jake just looked at him, knowing he couldn't say what he wanted to, couldn't tell Coach that he had enough to handle just being on this team. That even if he played the greatest season of his life, he didn't see how they could win more than two or three games, and that's if they were lucky.

He wanted to explain to the coach that he'd never been on a team this bad, and it was going to take all the love of soccer he had in him to give his all in every practice and in every game.

But he didn't say any of that. He didn't say a word. Because as much as Jake hated himself for thinking this, he couldn't help himself:

What about me?

FIVE

The second game of the season was worse than the first, even if the score wasn't.

Redwood, whose team wasn't nearly as good as Lincoln's, not even close, beat them 5–1. It was 4–0 at halftime, then 5–0 two minutes into the second half. This time it wasn't one of the best teams in Madison County going easy on them and trying not to run up the score. It was *Redwood*.

When Jake was still on Greenville last year, they'd called them "Deadwood." He couldn't remember for sure, but he thought they'd only won three games in the 11's. Maybe only two.

We can't even stay with these *guys,* Jake thought, as the second half seemed to take longer than one of those baseball playoff games that went so long your parents made you go to bed before it was over.

He'd told Coach Lord that with some world-class goalkeeping from Quinn, and a little luck, they could win a few games. But now Jake was starting to wonder if, no matter how many shots Quinn stopped, they were going to need the kind of luck that won people those Powerball lotteries.

Redwood took their first-string goalie out with five minutes left, even though the kid was pitching a shutout. Coach Lord had moved Reid McDonough up from defense by then, along with Mike Clark, just to shake things up a little. Maybe even help get Belmont one lousy goal.

Everybody joked that Reid had the hardest head on the team, maybe the hardest in the league. If there was an opportunity for him to head the ball, no matter where he was on the field, he would take it, whether it was the best way to get the ball going the other way or not.

"When he catches the ball just right," Quinn said one time, "I swear it sounds like a wood bat when you catch a pitch on the sweet spot."

Every time it happened, Reid would have this big smile on his face, as if it was the most fun he was going to have all day.

Jake was just looking for any kind of fun—looking to take away something good from this game—as he and Reid and Mike tried to put some pressure on the second-string goalie in the little time they had left. Reid on his right, Mike on his left. The way the play was opening up now, Jake thought Mike was going to be his best option.

Then the fullback on that side came up and spotted up on Mike, throwing a blanket over him.

But Jake had time to pull back on his pass and look at Reid. Sometimes that's all you got in soccer. One look. An open door closing fast. Suddenly there was this open patch of green between Reid and Redwood's fullback on his side.

Jake had beaten the stopper, but now their sweeper came in at him on an angle, making it impossible for Jake to skid the ball along the ground to Reid, as open as he was. So Jake improvised, getting his foot underneath the ball and launching a little floater before the sweeper could react to it.

Reid didn't even think about letting the ball land, even though he had the room and the time to do that.

He launched himself instead, with Jake thinking

that it wasn't just Reid's signature move, it was his *only* move.

Reid caught the ball with the top of his head exactly right and redirected it into the far corner. Redwood's backup keeper had no chance to do anything except watch.

Reid landed as hard on the ground as you did hitting the water with a belly flop. But he saw the ball go in, rolled over on his back, and started kicking his feet in the air and pumping his arms while the rest of the guys on their team came running for him.

Jake didn't join them.

He stayed where he was, the spot where he'd made the pass, and just watched. Feeling in that moment as if the celebration, for one goal at the end of another bad loss, involved somebody else's soccer team.

And maybe it did.

Jake was hoping Coach Lord would take him out then, put Cal in at center mid for the rest of the game.

But Coach left Jake in and took Reid out instead, letting him leave the game on a high note.

At least somebody gets to do that, Jake thought.

Coach replaced Reid with Kevin Crosby, whose giveaways in the first half, by Jake's unofficial count, had resulted in three Redwood goals.

"See if you can make Kevin's day the way you did Reid's," Coach said to Jake on the sideline.

"I'll try," Jake said. "But if I start feeding him the ball every time, he's going to know what I'm doing."

Coach said, "So what? Maybe it will make him mad enough to score a goal."

Jake tried to be creative about it, not make what he was doing obvious to everybody. And with less than a minute left, he found a way to give Kevin a perfect setup, even if it required a better acting job than anybody was going to do in the school play this year.

Redwood had cleared its bench by then, so the game was pretty much being played at their end of the field. One last time, Jake got behind the defense.

The shot was right there for him if he wanted it, even though the keeper had scrambled over on

Jake, trying to cut down the angle on him—or at least make him shoot before he was ready. Didn't matter. Jake had him, knew he could beat this kid with his eyes closed.

Only Jake wasn't out there to get himself a goal, he was out there to get one for Kevin, who was sitting just outside the goalie box, to Jake's right.

As open as anybody could ever be.

That was where the acting job came in.

Jake faked like he had slipped then, like it was a new move he had just invented on the fly: The Stuart Slip.

He went down on his right knee, but still managed to keep control of the ball with his left foot. Then he turned his body a little, got just enough on the ball to slide it over to Kevin, who had pretty much the whole goal to himself.

All he had to do was kick the ball.

He kicked it, all right.

Right back to Jake.

Pushed the ball so weakly across the front of the box that the kid in goal had plenty of time to recover, dive on it, jump to his feet, and kick it away down the field.

Jake watched until it finally came down. By the time it did, he was jogging alongside Kevin.

"Dude, you gotta shoot that," Jake said.

Not showing Kevin up, not even raising his voice, just letting him know.

"You shoot it," Kevin said. "Like you should have."

"I would have. I slipped."

Still acting.

By now the ball had gone out of bounds at midfield. Redwood's ball. Ten seconds left. The game wasn't coming back to this end of the field.

Kevin and Jake stopped.

"Do you think I'm that stupid?" Kevin said.

"No," Jake said. "But I do think you're a lot better of a player than you're showing."

"Don't you get it by now?" Kevin said. "I don't care what you think."

"I was just trying to make a play," Jake said.

"Go make your hero plays for somebody else," Kevin said.

They heard the ref blow his whistle three times now, meaning the game was over. Kevin tried to walk away from him. Still, Jake stayed with him.

He hadn't been able to make much of a difference while the game was still going on.

Maybe he could now that it was over.

"I'm not trying to be your hero or anybody else's," Jake said.

"Yeah, you are," Kevin said. "Everybody is."

"Dude. We're all on the same team."

"No," Kevin said. "We're really not."

They were in the back of the line now, moving toward the Redwood players. Before Jake could think of something else to say, Kevin looked over his shoulder and said, "We do have one thing in common when it comes to soccer."

"What?"

"Neither one of us can wait for these games to be over," Kevin said.

SIX

He couldn't talk about the team with Quinn—about how bad he thought it was—even though he talked about everything with Quinn.

Jake knew that if he did try to talk about everything he was feeling right now, there would be no way he could explain himself without sounding as if he were better than everybody else, that he was too good—or even too cool—to be playing with the rest of them.

Quinn included.

He wanted to believe things were going to get better, the way Quinn did, wanted to believe that in the worst way. Coach talked about how he could see improvement even though they couldn't see it on the scoreboard yet. But Jake wondered how Coach could possibly think that, knowing soccer the way he did, inside and out.

And maybe it didn't matter what anybody said. Jake was just going to have to suck it up, tell himself every day that if Coach and Quinn weren't going to hang their heads, then neither was he.

When he got home, he went straight up to his room, shut the door behind him, opened up the middle drawer of his desk, and got out the DVD of last year's championship game in the 11's that his dad had burned for him. He slid the DVD into his laptop.

Saw "Greenville 3, Franklin Park 2" come up in white letters against a black screen like it was the title of a home movie.

Jake's favorite home movie of all.

He'd played the game of his life that day, in the biggest game he'd had in his life so far.

Jake at center mid, Joe Healey at right mid, Paul Barberie on his left. Larry Campanelli in goal. Blake Marooney back there at stopper, swatting away shots like the world's greatest shot blocker in the NBA.

He watched on his computer screen as Greenville, he and all his buds from last season, always seemed to control the middle of the field, the way good teams did in soccer. Watched the way they only seemed to be playing at full speed when they saw an opening.

Watched the way everybody in white seemed to be thinking with the same soccer brain.

There was a moment near the end, the game still tied at 2, when Coach Ben Francis sent Jake down to take a corner kick. Jake watched himself lay the ball right in front of the goal, into the middle of the crowd of players there, the ball coming down perfectly out of the sky as if it had a chute attached to it.

He saw the ball coming down, Paul Barberie timing his jump just right, using his head the way Reid had today, and pounding that sucker so hard off the crossbar that Jake felt as if he could still hear the screaming sound of ball against metal—the worst sound in soccer unless you were a goalkeeper—in his bedroom.

There was a quick shot of Paul then, the camera right on him, hitting the sides of his head with his hands harder than the ball just had.

In his room now, Jake said in a soft voice, "Don't worry, Paulie. I got you."

And he did.

It was the last minute of the game when Jake came flying across midfield, doing a Maradona to get away from Franklin Park's center mid.

Already he could see Greenville's little striker, Johnny Gilman, clearing out ahead of him, knowing that this was one of those moments when, if he didn't clear out, Jake was going to run him over on his way toward the goal, run right up his back.

All this time later, watching the play unfold, Jake could still feel his heart start to beat faster.

Even knowing what was coming next.

Knowing that as he ran to his right that day, his back to Paul Barberie, he still knew exactly where Paul was, knew he was about to pass the Franklin Park fullback on that side of the field like he was a car running a stoplight.

On the screen Jake stopped now, planting his left foot, looking as if he was about to blast the kind of big shot they called a one-timer in hockey.

Only, he wasn't shooting. He was about to use

one of those extra sets of eyes to make a no-look pass across the field to Paul.

The goalie reacted, just not quickly enough. Like he was slowly figuring out that it wasn't a shot going wide to his right. It was a pass.

By the time he processed that and saw Paul closing in on him, it was too late. There was nothing for him to do as Paul controlled Jake's pass with his left foot and redirected it into the near corner for the goal that won the championship for Greenville.

It was then that Jake's dad pulled his camera away from the goal and put it on Jake. Then came the shot of Jake running and jumping his way across the field, almost on the same path his pass had just taken, arms stretched out wide, looking as happy as if he'd just scored the game-winner himself.

In all the important ways, he had.

It's why you play, Jake thought. *You play because sports can make you feel like this.*

Even if today he was wondering when he would ever feel that way again . . .

"Your favorite movie."

His mom.

Jake hadn't heard her come up the stairs, hadn't

heard his door open, didn't know how long she'd been watching him watch himself.

But when he turned around, she sure was smiling at him.

"It comes out the way I want it to every single time," he said. "Like *Miracle.*"

It was his all-time favorite sports movie, the true story of the US hockey team beating the Russians that time in the Olympics. He and Quinn agreed: If you turned on the television and *Miracle* was on, you always stayed with it, no matter where you were in the movie.

Same with Greenville 3, Franklin Park 2.

Jake hit the eject button on his laptop. The disc came sliding out, and he carefully put it back in its case, then spun his swivel chair around so he was facing his mom.

She was already sitting on the end of his bed, which meant she was settling in and wanted to talk.

"Tough one today," she said.

"They're all going to be tough ones, Mom."

"It's only been two games," she said. "Things will get better. I know you. You'll make them get better."

"Not enough."

"Wait a second," she said. "You can't decide how *this* movie will end in the first ten minutes."

Once his mom had her mind set on giving one of her pep talks, there was no stopping her.

"That's the problem—I do know how it's going to end," he said. "We're going to get smoked by every good team we play. Or it will be like today, and it won't even have to be a good team."

Grace Stuart put out a hand like a crossing guard at school. "Now I know you've heard me say this before, but sometimes in sports you've got to go through hard times to become the player you want to become."

"What I really want to become," Jake said, "is a Greenville Ram."

It got a laugh out of his mom, even though Jake wasn't trying to be funny.

"And I want to be nineteen again," she said. "And fit into the jeans I was wearing when I was nineteen."

"This is different."

"Not as much as you think, kiddo."

"If it was just me being stuck on a lousy team,

that would be one thing" Jake said. "But it's more than that, Mom."

"Had a feeling," she said.

"You always do."

"You know our deal," she said, smiling again. "What happens in Vegas stays in Vegas."

One of her favorite lines. And they both knew what she meant: He could confide in her. She never wanted Jake to hold back anything important.

So Jake just came out with it. "Now Coach wants me to babysit Kevin," he said.

There was a big quiet in the room then, one that seemed to last a long time, before his mom said, "By babysit, I assume you mean look out for him a little bit?"

Jake ducked his head, embarrassed, and said, "Something like that," and then he told her about the conversation he'd had with Coach Lord on the field that night. When he finished, he said, "But here's the thing—Kevin doesn't want my help or anybody else's. He told me today to stop trying to be his hero and leave him alone."

"You understand that he's only pushing everybody away right now because he's hurting so much?"

"Mom," Jake said. "I'm not thick. I get that. But it doesn't mean I can fix things between us." The next part just came out, like the words were shoving Kevin Crosby right out of his room. "Just like I can't fix this stupid team!"

His mom got up then, came over to Jake, and put a hand on his shoulder.

"Nobody's expecting you to fix it. At least not all by yourself."

"That's the way it feels sometimes, Mom. Like it's all on me."

There was a ball set on top of his clothes hamper. She picked it up now, bounced it off one knee, then the other, caught it. Old Mom was still good with the ball.

"That's because you've mostly been a winner so far in your life," she said. "But what you're going to find out, because we all find out sooner or later, is that there're ways of being a winner in sports that aren't always tied to the final score."

"Not when the final score is five to one."

"Kevin told you not to be his hero," she said. "Let's talk for a second about yours."

She already knew who they were. In soccer, it

was all the great playmakers. And Beckham. And Pelé. It was Derek Jeter in baseball, Steve Nash and Chris Paul in basketball. And even though he'd never seen him play when he was still playing, his all-time favorite hockey player, just from watching ESPN Classic, was Wayne Gretzky.

A center, of course.

Jake listed all those names for his mom now.

"What do all your sports heroes have in common?" she said.

Jake smiled, the way you did when you had the right answer for a teacher. "They make everybody around them better," he said.

"My work here is done," his mom said. "I knew you'd figure it out."

Jake said, "It's not like I didn't have a little help."

She turned for the door, then realized she was still holding the soccer ball in her hands. She dropped it toward the floor, caught it on her instep, flipped it with her right foot across the room to Jake, who caught it easily.

"One more assist for old Mom," she said.

SEVEN

Jake loved reading almost as much as he loved sports.

He tried to explain that to Quinn once and Quinn had looked at him like he was some kind of space alien.

"You mean, read when you don't have to?"

"Just for fun."

"You're telling me you'd rather read than game?"

That was the way Quinn talked about playing video games. You didn't *play* them. You *gamed*.

"You got it," Jake had said. "I'd rather read than game."

Quinn had thought that one over for a minute and finally said, "Well, call me crazy, but I still want to be your friend."

Once they were through with soccer on weekends, Quinn would be ready to game for the rest of the day. He didn't care whether it was *Tiger Woods* or *World Cup Soccer* or *Madden* or *NCAA Football*, as long as he had a controller in his hands and enough snacks to get him through the afternoon.

His favorite place to game was Jake's basement, because of the huge television down there. Sometimes Jake would leave him down there, go upstairs to check out a college football game or just to take a break. When he came back down the stairs, Quinn would still be there, concentrating as hard as he did when he was getting ready to face a shot in a real game.

Jake would wonder in those moments if Quinn even knew he'd left.

But no matter how much time the two of them spent together on weekends, Jake would always find time to read.

And his favorite place to do it was in The Stacks.

Jake loved going to the Belmont Public Library, scoping out a solitary corner for himself, upstairs or downstairs, in a chair or on the floor, and settling in with a good book.

He knew he could just as easily close the door to his room and read there. Because he had his own stacks—floor-to-ceiling shelves his dad had built into the walls by himself, carpentry being one of the many things he was good at. But there was something Jake just liked better about the shelves and stacks at the library, the cool feeling he got being surrounded by all those books.

The Belmont Public Library was even open on Sundays, between noon and four, and Jake planned to be there today as soon as Mrs. Johnson, the Sunday librarian, unlocked the front door. Quinn was coming over to the house later to hang out and game. But at five minutes to twelve, Jake got on his bike and rode the six blocks to the library.

He never came up a loser there.

There were no bad seasons there, not with books. Or bad teams. If you didn't like the one you were reading you could just go find another one you liked better.

If only soccer worked that way, Jake thought on the ride over.

Mrs. Johnson was at the front desk when he walked in. The clock behind her said it was 12:03.

Mrs. Johnson looked at him over her reading glasses and smiled. "Get stuck in traffic, Jake?"

Jake smiled back. "Got a late start. Mom and Dad took me out for breakfast after church."

"I thought you might have a game."

Jake said, "We usually only play on Saturdays."

"How's the team doing this year?" she said, obviously trying to be friendly, not knowing it was a little like asking Jake how his trip to the dentist's office had gone.

"Not too good," he said, then remembered his manners and thanked her for asking.

And headed up the stairs.

Jake didn't always go to the same section. He didn't like just one author. Carl Hiaasen was one of his favorites. He liked John H. Ritter's baseball books a lot. But he liked old-time books, too, ones that his parents—his dad, especially—had told him about, or had even read to him and along with him at night. So he read the baseball books by a writer named John R. Tunis. And the Hardy Boys mysteries. And "science-adventure" stories about this kid Rick Brant. And the sports books that his dad said he'd loved the most when he was a boy, about Chip Hilton.

Jake just looked for good stories, basically, ones that would keep him turning the pages, ones that would take him places he'd never been before.

Today he was up in Sports Fiction, on the second level of the library, having pulled a Chip Hilton he hadn't read yet: *Hardcourt Upset*. Now the only question was where he wanted to sit and read it. He walked over to the balcony, which wrapped all the way around the second floor, and looked down, trying to decide which of his favorite spots was going to be his personal reading room until it was time to go meet Quinn.

Sometimes, if the library was crowded, he'd just stay up here and plop himself down on the carpet. Sometimes, if the place was as empty as it was now, he'd pick out a sofa or chair in one of the lounge areas.

Which was where he spotted Kevin Crosby.

Jake couldn't see what Kevin was reading. But even from up here he could see Kevin was concentrating hard, the same way Jake would when he'd lose himself in a good book right there in the same chair.

Jake wasn't sure what to do. It was silly not to let him know he was up here. Or maybe not. Maybe Kevin just wanted to be left alone in the library the way he wanted to be left alone on a soccer field.

Or maybe here they could find out they did have something in common, that if it wasn't soccer, it could at least be that they both liked books.

Man, Jake thought, *this guy is tough. I never seem to know what the right move is.*

Kevin looked up then, almost as if he could hear Jake talking to himself.

Jake smiled, embarrassed, like he'd been caught grabbing a snack before dinner, and gave him a little wave.

Only Kevin didn't smile back. Or wave. Or motion for him to come down. His response was to slam his book shut, the sound like a thunderclap in the quiet library.

Then he got up out of the chair, glared up at Jake one last time, disappeared into the stacks for a moment, and walked past Mrs. Johnson and out the front door.

EIGHT

Jake didn't say anything to Kevin about what had happened at the library. Didn't say anything on the bus Monday morning, at their lockers when they got to school, in the two morning classes they shared.

What would have been the point, anyway?

Jake couldn't *ever* say the right thing with Kevin. He couldn't ever *do* the right thing, even when he was giving him a perfect set-up pass in soccer. So why even bother telling him that he hadn't followed him to the library, that he was just there to be alone with books the way Kevin obviously was?

Jake did try to explain all that to Quinn at lunch.

"Every time I put my hand out to the guy, it's like he slaps it away," Jake said.

Quinn grinned. "You're just mad because you can't find anything that works with him."

"Uh, that would be a 'no,'" Jake said. "This isn't about me."

"You sure about that?"

"What's that supposed to mean?" Jake said.

"It means you're making a bigger deal out of this than it actually is," Quinn said. "I'm not talking about what happened to Kevin's mom, 'cause that's the biggest deal possible. I mean what's going on between him and you."

"That's what I'm trying to tell you," Jake said. "There *is* no him and me."

"No, dude. There is. It's like you've turned this into some kind of competition. Like some game you're trying to win. Only he won't play."

"Coach is the one who started this," Jake said. "He told me to try and help the guy."

"Well, at least you gave it a full shot," Quinn said, being sarcastic in a Quinn way. "Like, two whole days."

Jake said, "You didn't see the look he gave me at the library."

"Oooh," Quinn said, "a mean look. I'm trembling with fear."

"You're saying this is my fault?"

"No," Quinn said. "I'm just saying you'll figure something out."

The bell rang then. And for once, Jake couldn't wait to get to his next class.

All you had to do there was open your book to figure things out.

They were like a different team the next Saturday against Warrenburg.

This time they weren't getting blown out in the first half, or just trying to hang in there until they did get blown out in the second.

This time they were winning the game.

Warrenburg wasn't one of the top teams in their league. But they weren't one of the worst, either. Last season they'd been good enough in the 11's to make it all the way to the semifinals of the league's postseason tournament, and Jake knew they were 1–1 this season.

But now they were down 3–1 to Belmont twenty minutes into the second half. And whether you were playing in the game or just watching it, you knew there were two reasons why: Jake and Quinn.

Jake was controlling the game and Quinn was doing everything except stand on his head to make saves. Jake's dad was a great tennis player, and he had told him once that when tennis players got going really good and felt as if every shot they hit was going to be a winner, they were "in the zone."

Today it was as if both Jake and Quinn were in the zone.

Jake had scored Belmont's first two goals in the first half, and had just fed Cal Morris for their third. But it wasn't just scoring today, because good soccer was always more than that. Sometimes you could dominate the game without getting anywhere near the other team's keeper.

Today, with a chance to win the game, not playing from 5–0 behind or 6–0 behind for a change, Jake was doing what all the best center mids, and all his heroes in the other sports, were supposed to do: He was making the game go through him.

Today he wasn't just trying to bring Kevin

Crosby into the action; he was doing that with everybody. He wasn't just getting himself a goal at what the basketball announcers called "garbage time." No. Today Jake was playing the way he knew he was meant to play all day long. The middle of the field was his again, whether he was starting Belmont's offense or stopping Warrenburg's before they could start it.

For the first time this season, Jake's teammates were *reading* him. They were ready when the passes came, which meant that the passes were connecting for a change. And every couple of minutes, at least it seemed that way to Jake, they were putting more pressure on the Warrenburg defense—stopper, sweeper, fullbacks, goalkeeper—all of them.

Jake was completely caught by surprise: This game actually felt like last season. Soccer was fun again.

But not for everybody.

Kevin wasn't into the game, wasn't showing the kind of emotion the rest of the guys were showing, especially when Quinn would make another save that looked like something out of one of his video games.

But at least Kevin wasn't hurting them. Jake wasn't even worried when Coach Lord decided to put him back in at right mid with five minutes left. He still had Cal with him on his left, and Cal was having his best game by far. The two of them were ready to run some clock, try not to force things, play keep-away in the middle of the field for as long as they could.

The ball went over to Cal and then came back to Jake. Before he could give it back to Cal, though, Warrenburg's right middie came up on him. Two other guys ran at Jake. So he wheeled around, saw Kevin was open over in front of the Belmont bench and sent the ball over there instead.

As he did, not wanting to take any chances, he just waved Kevin in the general direction of the Warrenburg goal, telling him to carry the ball himself, no one was near him at the moment.

Only, Kevin acted as if they were playing a game of hot potato. As soon as the ball came to him, he kicked it right back to Jake, the way he had in front of the goal that day at practice.

The result was much worse this time.

Warrenburg's center mid was a streak then, a

blur, intercepting Kevin's pathetic pass with ease. Now he was the one turning defense into offense, the way Jake had been doing all game long, before Jake could even react to the action going the other way.

The ball went up to Warrenburg's striker, back to the center middie, then over again to the striker who was cutting behind Reid and Mike Clark, in alone on Quinn.

No chance for Quinn to make a hero save this time.

The kid buried the ball in the upper corner and just like that it was a one-goal game.

Jake had tried to catch up to the play, but couldn't. He just watched helplessly as the whole thing unfolded. When the ball was behind Quinn, all Jake could do was spin around, a Maradona spin without the ball, put his hands on his hips, and try to glare a hole right through Kevin the way he had done to Jake at the library.

Kevin just shrugged, put his hands out, and turned away.

No big deal.

Now Jake was running in Kevin's direction. Not

about to let this one go. He was going to say something before Kevin lost them a game they'd been winning all day, acting as if he didn't give a rip one way or the other . . .

And then he stopped.

He knew Coach Lord wasn't going to stop him. Jake knew this was what Coach had talked about—getting on Kevin the way he wanted to right now, in the worst way.

In fact, this was *exactly* what Coach had talked about.

But Jake couldn't do it.

Could not.

He could make a ball do almost anything he wanted in soccer, could kick with either foot, could kick long and short and accurately. Jake just couldn't bring himself to kick Kevin Crosby when he was this far down.

No matter how much he wanted to blow off some steam.

And no matter what he said to Kevin, Jake knew it wasn't going to change him and it wasn't going to change what the score was now, and it sure wasn't going to help Belmont win this game. Jake wanted this game bad. Knew he was going to have to play now, as hard as he had been all day. Belmont's comfort zone, their two-goal cushion, was gone. They were one mistake away from being tied. Games changed that fast in sports, and then it was like a whole new game had started.

It was like a line he'd heard from Mike Tyson one time while watching an HBO show on how he'd wrecked his boxing career, pretty much wrecked his whole life. But when he was young and still the heavyweight champion, he was talking about this guy Biggs he was going to fight, and how the experts were saying Biggs had a pretty good plan to beat him.

"Everybody's got a plan till they get hit," Mike Tyson said.

Now Belmont had been hit. Right before Jake put the ball back in play, he turned around and looked behind him at Quinn, knowing that if he could draw confidence from anybody, it would be from his best bud.

Quinn ran out from the goal when he saw Jake staring down at him, pointed a finger at Jake, then pointed one at himself, as if to say, *We still got this*.

Like it was the two of them gaming against the whole Warrenburg team.

Somehow Belmont managed to regroup and play the next few minutes in the Warrenburg end. Cal even got off a couple of good shots, one missing the top corner of the goal by a foot.

Then it happened.

Warrenburg's right middie got out on a sprint, sailing down the right sideline, nobody stopping him. Reid seemed to have him lined up, but then just as the Warrenburg kid ducked his shoulder and tried to get around him the way you tried to get around the corner on a drive in basketball, Reid got his feet tangled up and went down.

When Mike came over to try to cover, one of their strikers filled the open spot in the middle of the field.

The right middie passed it over to him.

Twenty yards behind the play, Jake thought, *They're going to tie this stinking game, with thirty stinking seconds left on the clock.*

Only Quinn O'Dell thought otherwise.

He made himself wait until the kid with the ball committed himself. And when the kid tried to hit one low and to Quinn's right, going for the corner, Quinn timed his dive perfectly, laid himself out, extending his arms as far as they would go.

He got his two gloved hands on the ball, seemed to have a perfect grip on it.

But then he didn't, as he hit the ground so hard that Jake saw the ball start to come loose, knowing that if it did it was going to roll behind Quinn and into the net.

It didn't come loose, because somehow Quinn managed to reach up with his right hand and pin the ball to his head and keep it there.

Pin it the way David Tyree of the Giants had with the greatest catch in the history of the Super Bowl, when the Giants had upset the Patriots to break up their undefeated season.

The ball wasn't getting behind Quinn, no matter what.

The Warrenburg players closest to him stopped then, as if they couldn't believe what had just happened right in front of them.

They might have stopped, but Quinn O'Dell kept playing.

Boy, did he keep playing.

He popped up like a jack-in-the-box, squared himself, booted the ball as high and hard as he ever had in his life, half the length of the field at Belmont Middle School to where Jake was waiting for it, as if this were a play they'd called in a pickup touch football game. As if Quinn had told Jake to go long and he'd get it to him.

Jake was in full stride before Quinn's foot hit the ball. He could have gone all the way to the goal, past the flat-footed Warrenburg defenders who seemed as stunned—or as beaten—as the guys on their offense were in front of Quinn.

Jake knew there was one more goal waiting for him at the other end of the field if he wanted it.

He didn't.

He just wanted the game to be over.

So he pulled up, dribbled toward the Belmont bench, right at Coach Lord, reversed his field, played keep-away all by himself this time, in the zone to the end. He dribbled the ball until he heard the ref blow his whistle twice and then again, meaning it was over.

Belmont 3, Warrenburg 2.

Jake ran then with the ball under his arm toward

their goal, wanting to give the ball to Quinn. When he got there, Quinn was on his back, arms crossed in front of him, eyes closed.

"Okay, are you sleeping?" Jake said. "Or did the excitement of making that save kill you?"

It was as if that was what Quinn had been waiting for, because he opened his eyes then, smiled at Jake, sat up.

"No, that's what I'm trying to show you, dude," Quinn said. "We ain't dead yet!"

Jake wasn't so sure. Wasn't sure how happy he was supposed to feel. Wasn't sure how many more days like this there were going to be.

But for now, he had to admit it: This one would have to do.

NINE

The next two practices after the Warrenburg game were their best of the season—guys smiling again, having fun, a lot of chatter the whole time, everybody acting as if the season was starting all over again.

Everybody except Kevin, of course.

No matter how much Coach Lord tried to get him into the same kind of groove, he still seemed to be playing at a speed slower than everybody else. Jake sometimes felt as if the rest of the team were passing Kevin like he was a car on the highway going too slow in the right lane.

But he was the only one. The rest of the guys couldn't wait until Saturday. It still only took one win in sports to get everybody this excited.

And the one who was the most excited of all was

Jake Stuart. He was actually starting to believe that maybe he could do what Coach wanted him to do and rally the whole team around him. Not do everything all by himself. Just do that one thing.

After Thursday's practice, Jake even went out into the backyard after supper, to the far corner where his mom and dad had not only put up a goal for him, but had hung a net behind it in the trees, so Jake didn't have to keep chasing the ball into the woods when he was out here by himself.

Jake didn't always feel as if he were alone out here. Sometimes he would look up at his parents' bedroom window and see the shadow of his mom in the light, standing there watching him.

But when it was just him and a ball and the goal, the game was always the same: Penalty kick in a shoot-out to win the World Cup. Oh, yeah. Jake knew enough soccer history to know that there had been World Cup finals that had come down to PK's. He knew it had happened after Zidane's head butt and that Italy had won the shoot-out.

Before that, there was the Italy vs. Brazil game in the first World Cup played in the United States.

The Italian player, Baggio, had scored an amazing five goals in the previous three games. But now Italy and Brazil had ended the game tied and were locked in a shoot-out. It all came down to Baggio, Italy's star player. The dream moment for any soccer player.

One kick for everything. One shot to keep your team alive.

Yet Baggio had missed.

Jake wanted that same chance.

One kick.

He set the ball down on his mark, twelve yards from the goal, about to make the one kick that everybody would remember. The one that he'd been making out here for as long as *he* could remember.

Not the kind of pass that he'd made to win the championship of the 11's for Greenville last year. Oh no, this was was the World Cup final. Tonight he'd decided it was the US against Pelé's best Brazil team—and both teams had gone through the shoot-out and they were still tied and now it came down to one shooter at a time. Pelé had missed.

The US coach told Jake to go make the shot

that would win the United States its first World Cup.

They were in the Rose Bowl, just because to Jake that was the biggest place in all of sports, maybe because he'd seen the Baggio kick there about a hundred times.

Jake pictured the goalkeeper from Brazil bouncing on his toes, rocking back and forth, ready to pounce.

He heard the ref blow the whistle.

Knew where he was going with his shot tonight— upper corner to the keeper's right.

Jake took a deep breath, stepped into his shot, and hit it perfectly, feeling like a field goal kicker in football who knew he'd nailed the game-winning kick as soon as his foot hit the ball. In the night quiet of the backyard, there were just the two sounds now: the ball hitting the inside of Jake's right foot and then the sweet sound of the ball rippling the net in the corner, right where Jake had aimed the sucker.

Jake heard the roar of the crowd then, 100,000 people cheering for him.

There wasn't going to be a kick like this for him

this year, even if he was still in the glow of the Warrenburg game. Belmont wasn't going to get anywhere near the championship game of the 12's.

But someday, Jake told himself.

Someday.

TEN

They lost 6–2 to Newbury on Saturday when Newbury scored the last five goals of the game.

Then they lost 7–4 to Easton the next Saturday, with Quinn twisting his knee right at the end of the first half and unable to play the rest of the game.

So much for building on the win over Warrenburg.

So much for having fun, Jake thought. So much for rallying the troops. Or being better than they were supposed to be. Two Saturdays later it was as if the Warrenburg game had never happened.

It didn't matter what Jake did against Easton, on offense or defense. Belmont was getting beaten all over the field and there was nothing he could do to stop it. Even Quinn, before he got hurt, was having his worst game so far, taking chances he normally didn't take, as if he were trying too hard to make something good happen for his team.

So it was already 4–2 for Easton when one of their strikers landed on Quinn's right knee. And even though Bo Doherty, one of their starting fullbacks, had been itching to get a shot as goalkeeper, he looked scared to death once he put on the jersey and actually had to stand in there.

Bo gave up two goals in the first two minutes of the second half, then another a few minutes later. Just like that, they were getting blown out again. Another no-chance, beatdown Saturday.

Look at me, Jake thought.

The great difference maker.

It had taken two games for them to turn back into one of those loser teams you saw in soccer movies. Except in the movies the team always found a way to get good by the end. Jake realized now that wasn't going to happen with his team, that he wasn't going to be able to lift a team the way Nash could in basketball, the way Chris Paul had lifted the Hornets his first couple of years. In basketball, it was only four other guys you had to make better. In basketball, one guy could control the ball enough to control the game.

Not in soccer. Too many players, on both sides of the ball.

Too big a field and too big a job.

When he finally heard the whistles ending the Easton game, he walked slowly to the sideline and got in the back of the line for the handshake, in front of Coach Lord.

"Hang in there, pal," Coach said. "We just hit another bump in the road."

"No," Jake said, turning his head enough that only Coach could hear him. "We're off the road and into the ditch and we're not getting out."

He turned back around as the line started to move.

"We just have to work harder," Coach Lord said.

"I'm working my butt off, Coach," Jake said. "And we're still one-and-four."

"I see how hard you're working," Coach said. "But we've just got to put this one behind us . . ."

"And the one before that."

". . . and look ahead, because we've got some winnable games coming up."

He put his hand on Jake's shoulder, but Jake shrugged it off.

"On what planet?" Jake said under his breath.

Then one by one he was telling the guys on the Easton team how well they'd played, how they deserved it, have a great season, maybe we'll see you in the playoffs. Even though that was a laugh—there were ten teams in their league and the top eight made the playoffs, and no way were they good enough to get to number eight.

When he was done shaking hands, Jake went over to where Quinn was sitting on the bench, the huge icepack back on his knee, and asked if he still wanted to come over later, or if he just wanted to go home and put his leg up for the rest of the day.

"I can still game," Quinn said.

"I'm curious," Jake said, happy to be talking about anything except soccer. "What would it take for you *not* to game?"

Quinn frowned, as if he were really thinking it over. Then his face brightened. "You mean other than one of those power failures that takes out half the East Coast?" he said.

Quinn said he'd be over to Jake's house about three. His mom was running him over to the doctor's first because their family doctor had offered to take a look at the knee even though it was a Saturday.

Jake picked up his ball, walked around the fence to where his mom was waiting for him. His dad was out of town on business until the middle of next week. Jake figured his dad had caught a break, not having to sit through another loss like this one.

No worries, though.

There were plenty more losses to come, and Jake figured they were all going to look pretty much the same.

Jake's mom said, "Ask you a question?"

"Please don't make it a hard one."

"When you hang your head like that, are you ever afraid you're going to scrape your nose on the ground?"

Jake knew she was doing what she always did at times like this, which meant trying to get a smile out of him. She admitted to Jake once that trying to get just one smile out of him after a bad loss sometimes felt like the biggest job she'd have all day.

But on this day, Jake didn't even look up.

"I don't want to do this today," he said.

"You're absolutely right. I quit, no point in even trying," she said. "This is it, a new world's record, the crabbiest you've ever looked after soccer. Except perhaps for that time when your shorts fell down when you were six."

She wasn't quitting even if she said she was. Moms never did. If you were in a lousy mood, they'd throw everything they had at you trying to get you out of it. If they didn't *know* why you were in a lousy mood, they'd get on a mission to find out.

"Mom," he said, "please give it up."

Now he looked up. Into a smile, of course.

"You want to hear about some of my worst days in soccer?" she said. "You don't remember this, but when I couldn't get you to sleep when you were little, I'd start telling you about my career."

"No, thank you."

"Okay, how about we do it this way? I'll pay you for a smile."

"How much?"

"Now that right there is sad," his mom said. "Finding out, once again, that everybody has a price, even Mr. Mope Face."

Jake said, "Okay, I give up, I'll smile." Then he looked up at her, hooked his thumbs into his mouth, pulled them up into a fake smile. "There," he said. "Are you happy?"

She put her thumbs in her mouth then, trying to make the same fright-face back at him.

Jake couldn't help it. He laughed now. Laughed and actually meant it. "You're a great mom," he said. "But you make the world's worst clown."

"Least I didn't play like one," she said, saying it under her breath but wanting him to hear.

"Oh, *that's* nice."

Grace Stuart said, "Just keepin' it real, dude."

Jake said, "We *did* play like clowns. Though if you think about it, that's pretty insulting to actual clowns."

"True dat," his mom said.

"Oh no," Jake said. "Please don't try to talk like that."

Then his mom was grabbing the ball away from

him, imitating the moment when Jake had slipped trying to take a shot in the first half, had his feet go out from under him like he was a guy in a cartoon slipping on a banana peel.

They were laughing together now, too loudly and probably too soon after a loss like this, though most of the other players and their parents were already gone by then. Jake didn't care. All of a sudden he felt a little less bad, which maybe was the best thing your parents could do for you.

As they made the turn toward the parking lot his mom said, wait, she wanted to imitate that shot one more time. Jake begged her not to, but she said no, she had to get it exactly right. But this time she was the one who slipped, ended up sitting down hard on the ground. Then the two of them were laughing again, louder than before, his mom pulling him into a hug when he helped her to her feet.

It was in that moment that Jake looked over her shoulder, to the hill behind her where parents would lay their blankets sometimes and watch games.

Kevin Crosby was sitting up there, alone, obviously waiting for his dad, staring at Jake again. Only this time it wasn't the library and Kevin didn't have the kind of face on that made it seem as if he half-wanted to fight Jake.

This time it was about the saddest face Jake had ever seen, like Kevin had his nose pressed to some imaginary window, like he was on the outside of something looking in.

The boy who'd lost his mom was watching Jake be happy with his.

ELEVEN

After church on Sunday morning, Jake looked up Kevin's address in the Belmont Middle School handbook and found that it was on Maple Street. Three blocks away. Short bike ride.

He told his mom he was going out and he'd be back in time for lunch.

"You going over to Quinn's?"

"Nah."

She looked up at the kitchen clock and said, "This is way too early for the library to be open. Unless they're letting you open it yourself now."

"Not going to the library today."

Jake had his hand on the doorknob, just wanting to get his bike out of the garage. Just do it, before he lost his nerve.

"I thought I might take a ride over to Kevin's, actually. He lives just over on Maple."

She was about to take a sip of her coffee, but held her cup where it was, a few inches from her mouth.

"Kevin, huh?" she said. "Did you two set something up for today? Should I call his parents—his dad?"

"No!"

It came out as loud as if he'd dropped something on the floor.

"Okaaay."

"I just—" Jake stopped. "I just feel like it's time we talked some stuff out."

"Did something else happen between the two of you that I should know about?"

Jake shook his head, tried to smile, even if he knew it had nothing behind it. "Maybe I'm trying to *make* something happen," Jake said.

He took his time, rode around for a while before making his way down to Maple Street. He found number 127, a big white house with white shutters and a bright red front door. Through Quinn, Jake knew that Kevin had two older sisters, both in college. So now it was just Kevin and his dad at home.

Maybe that's why Jake had expected the house to be smaller than it was.

Jake stood on the sidewalk, wondering how quiet it must be on the other side of that red door.

He laid his bike in the grass, walked up the brick path, saw that the door had a big metal knocker on it, banged that a couple of times, not too hard, feeling first-day-of-school nervous as he did.

There was no car in the driveway, but that didn't mean anything—their garage door was closed. Jake still found himself half-hoping that there was nobody home.

Then he heard footsteps from inside, heard Kevin's dad saying that he'd get it. The door opened and there Mr. Crosby was, a tall man with dark glasses wearing a Princeton sweatshirt and jeans.

He smiled and said, "What can I do for you?"

Jake said, "Is Kevin here?"

"Wait a second," Mr. Crosby said, like he was taking a closer look at him. "You're Jake, right? From the team?"

"Yes sir. Jake Stuart."

"Man, there are times when you're all we've got this season, Jake. You're some player."

"Thanks. Not that it's doing us much good."

"Well, hang in there," he said, motioning for Jake to come in. "In sports you compete as hard as you can and maybe good things can still happen."

By now Jake just figured it was something that parents were programmed to say, something on everybody's parental advice shuffle.

When they were in the front hall, at the bottom of a long winding stairway, Mr. Crosby said, "Was Kevin expecting you?"

Jake said, "Nah, I was just riding by and remembered you guys lived on this street. I thought I'd drop in."

In a quiet voice Mr. Crosby said, "Between us? I'm glad you did, son. He hasn't had many visitors lately."

He called upstairs to Kevin then, told him he had a visitor.

They sat in Kevin's room.

Kevin was in the swivel chair at his desk, his computer behind him, the screen saver a picture of him and a woman who Jake assumed was his mom.

Jake was on the edge of the bed, checking out the room, noticing right away there were no posters on the walls. But there was a small TV set, making Jake totally jealous since his own parents had informed him, practically from birth, that he could get a TV in his room if he got one for himself at college.

The rest of Kevin Crosby's room was filled with books.

There were books everywhere. Jake thought Kevin didn't need to go to a library; he was practically living in one. Jake had a lot of books in his room, too, but he wasn't even close to Kevin. There were *three* tall bookcases in here, books on the table next to Kevin's bed, even books stacked on the floor in the corner.

At least they gave Jake something to talk about, so they didn't have to just sit there staring at each other. He made a gesture that tried to take in every book in the room, saying, "You've *read* all these?"

"Most."

"How do you have the time, with school and all?"

Kevin lifted his shoulders, let them drop. "I've got time."

"Got a favorite writer? I—"

"I just like to read," Kevin said, cutting him off, almost like he wanted to change the subject.

The uncomfortable silence returned and Jake was starting to second-guess himself for coming to this place, feeling totally *out* of place.

This wasn't a soccer field, where Jake always felt comfortable, always felt as if he was on his own turf, even when a game was turning to slop. Wasn't school or the bus, with other people around. It was just the two of them, nobody else around, no sounds coming from the rest of the too-big, too-quiet house.

With absolutely nothing to say to each other.

Except that Jake had come here to say *something*.

Kevin beat him to it.

"So what do you want?"

"I was just out riding around," Jake said. "I like to do that sometimes. My parents even let me ride into town. Then I remembered Quinn telling me you lived on Maple."

Kevin shook his head. "That's not why you're here."

Jake smiled. "You got me," he said.

"So why *are* you here?"

Just put it out there, chicken wing.

"I just thought we might hang out or whatever," Jake said. "Go grab Quinn and do something."

He said it, had come over here to say it, knowing it was something guys never talked about. Hanging out. Even when Jake had first moved to Belmont, it wasn't something he and Quinn had ever discussed, that they were going to hang out, be buds.

It was something you just *did*.

"Hang out," Kevin said.

"I mean, I've got no big plan. We could game at my house—I've got a pretty cool big screen in the basement. Or go over to Quinn's. Maybe mess around with a ball in my backyard. I've got a goal back there. It's pretty decent. Like I said, whatevs."

Kevin stood up. Somehow in here, even in a bedroom twice the size of Jake's, he looked a lot bigger than he did on a soccer field. Maybe because he'd spent the whole season trying to make himself invisible.

He went and stood at the window and looked

out at his own backyard, didn't turn back around as he said, "You came here because you feel sorry for me. It's why you do everything. If you didn't feel sorry, you wouldn't even *talk* to me."

"No," Jake said, "it's not like that." He cleared his throat, the way he did when he was nervous and had to say something in class. "I mean, I'm not gonna lie, maybe a little bit, maybe at first, anyway. I'm not even gonna pretend I understand what happened to you, because I'd sound dumber than dirt if I did." At least finally saying what he had come here to say. "But we're on the same team, we ride the same bus, we live in the same neighborhood. Dude, I just figured we *ought* to be hanging out."

Now Kevin turned around. "Did Coach put you up to this, too?"

Stung, Jake said, "Why would you even think something like that?"

"So he did."

"No," Jake said. "Man, that's just plain *wrong*."

Trying to keep his voice calm, trying not to lose his temper, even though he couldn't believe that he'd come all the way over here to have this guy still act like this much of a jerk.

"Some pity time to go with the pity shots you try to get me on the field?"

"*No!*"

Now Jake was standing, too. Feeling his fists clench.

"What do you want to do next, loan me your mom?"

Wow.

Jake said, "That's a dumb thing to say."

"Maybe not as dumb as you coming over here."

"Maybe not!" Jake said.

Neither one of them could stop this now. Jake felt as if they were both rolling down a hill.

"So why don't you just leave?" Kevin said. "How many times do I have to tell you to leave me alone?"

"Why, so you can sit here and feel sorrier for yourself than you already do?"

Kevin Crosby nodded. "I knew that's what you thought. What everybody thinks. I just didn't know whether you'd admit it or not."

Jake said, "Man, this is so messed up. I just came over because I thought we could be friends. I didn't want everything to go all weird like this."

"You know what's *really* weird?" Kevin said. "I don't feel nearly as sorry for myself as you do for yourself."

"Okay, that makes *no sense.*"

"Yeah, it does."

"I feel sorry for myself. Right."

"You do," Kevin said. "Because you're stuck on a team with guys like me."

"Right," Jake said again, trying to make it come out even more sarcastic this time.

"I *am* right. The one who really needs a pity party is you, Stuart. Not me."

TWELVE

Jake had wanted to come back at him one more time. Wanted to ask him, seriously, why he was acting as if Jake had come over to trash his room, rather than to be a friend.

But he was smart enough to know that both of them had said way more than enough today.

So he had walked out of Kevin's bedroom without another word, taking the steps two at a time as he went back downstairs to the front hall. He didn't even think about finding Mr. Crosby to say goodbye, just opened the red door and slammed it behind him harder than he meant to, and got on his bike and rode away.

This time, on the way home, he rode fast.

He wanted to get away from this sad house and the sad kid inside it as quickly as he possibly could.

What Jake couldn't get away from, no matter how fast he pedaled, was the idea that Kevin might be right.

Somehow he was able to get Quinn to leave the basement for some one-on-one action in the backyard.

Usually that only happened if they had been having some kind of gaming marathon and Jake kept beating him.

But today Quinn wanted to go out after only about an hour because he wanted to test his knee.

"Is that okay with the doctor and your mom?" Jake said.

"Dubes," Quinn said.

In Quinn-speak, that meant "dubious."

"Well, then, maybe we shouldn't. I don't want you to do something and really mess it up and be out for a month. Because if that happens, other teams are going to start putting basketball scores on us."

"I'm sorry," Quinn said, "did you want to know if it was all right with my mom, or do you want to *be* my mom?"

"Just don't get crazy on me," Jake said.

"I just want to stuff you a few times and get my mojo back."

"In that case, it's on."

They went out to the goal and took turns shooting. Jake thought of himself as a pretty decent keeper, and he knew he could be even better if he decided to switch positions. More than that, he thought that if Quinn came out and played one of the attacking positions in soccer, he'd be the second-best player on their team.

After Jake.

Quinn didn't have Jake's speed or vision or feel for the game, but Jake knew he made up for that with his heart, because he hated to lose as much as Jake did, even if he didn't let it show the way Jake did.

Though today, Kevin Crosby had made it pretty clear that he thought Jake had been showing it *too* much.

What they did today was invent their own soccer version of H-O-R-S-E. They didn't make it so you had to aim for the same part of the goal, but if one of them made a shot from the keeper's left, the other guy had to shoot from the same spot.

If one of them called "left foot" before shooting, the other guy had to shoot with his left foot, too.

They both knew, of course, that Quinn didn't have nearly the left foot that Jake did. That's why when Quinn got ahead, Jake started going to his left foot every time.

"That is dirty," Quinn said when Jake finally came back to beat him with a low left-foot shot to Quinn's left, the ball shooting past his buddy like a hard ground ball past an infielder.

Jake grinned. "I'm sure you would have had it if you weren't practically playing with a broken leg."

Quinn said, "I'm just letting you win, so you can have one day when you actually look like you're having fun playing soccer again."

Jake had just retrieved the ball from the corner of the net. Now he stopped in front of Quinn and said, "Seriously . . . are you saying I *don't* look like I'm having fun?"

"Aw man," Quinn said. "Don't get that look on me."

"What look?"

"The look like you're going all serious."

"I'm not going all serious, I'm just asking a question."

"But you have to admit: It's a *serious* question."

"Are you gonna answer it anytime before, like, Tuesday?"

"Yes," Quinn said. "Or is it no? No, definitely no. You're not having fun."

Jake said, "But I'm trying as hard as I ever did. Maybe harder than I ever did."

"Not trying to have fun."

"I didn't know you had to try to do that."

"Apparently, this season you do," Quinn said.

"Let me ask you a question," Jake said. "Are *you* having fun?"

Quinn sat down in the grass now, like he knew Jake was digging in on this, and there was nothing he could do about it unless he wanted to go home.

"Yeah," he said. "I am."

"So you're down with us being probably the worst team in the league?"

"Didn't say that. I hate getting waxed like this as much as you do. But I still have fun playing. No matter what the score is, I'm not gonna hang back there in front of the goal and act all pouty like somebody made me go sit in a corner, or like my parents gave me one of those time-outs they used to give me."

Jake sat down next to him. Quinn made a motion for the ball. Jake gave it to him, and Quinn lay back using the ball like a pillow.

"Am I acting that way?" Jake said.

"Truth?"

"Truth."

"Yeah, that's exactly how you're acting."

He remembered what Kevin said to him now, and how he'd said it. "You think the other guys think I think I'm better than everybody else?"

Quinn said, "I don't know what they think. Don't care, really, because I know nobody knows you like I do. I'm just sayin'."

"But sayin' *what*?"

Without much effort, so quick it surprised Jake, Quinn flipped the ball into the air as he was sitting up and headed it into the goal, looking as happy as if he'd just scored to beat Greenville.

"I guess I'm saying that you got to ask yourself

why you play, is all. I play to win, you know I do. I play to win when we're gaming. Dude, I even get excited when I can answer one of those silly questions on the inside of Snapple caps. But more than that, I play to *play*."

He turned now, facing Jake head-on. "I just love to play, no matter how many balls end up behind me. Yesterday, even before I dinged my knee, I knew I was playing lousy, that I was so far out of my game somebody needed to draw a map for me to find my way back. And I knew that no way we were coming back on those guys. But you know what killed me more than anything, worse than the way I was playing? *Not* playing."

"Maybe I'm different."

"Nah, that's the thing. You're not. Man, I watch you when you start to dish out there. I don't even need to see your face, I know that when you get going like that, you're exactly where you're s'posed to be."

Jake knew enough about himself to know that that part was true. It was just that he wasn't getting that feeling nearly enough. It was one of the problems in soccer, especially when the other team was controlling the flow of the game: There was too much downtime.

It felt like he was having a whole season of downtime.

"Maybe sometimes I've got too much time to think," Jake said.

"Never a good thing with you."

"No doubt."

Now Quinn surprised him again. He went and picked up the ball and when he brought it back, he bicycled the ball from behind him and into the net. A Pelé move if there ever was one. And Quinn had made it look easy.

"I didn't know you could do that," Jake said.

"Lot of stuff you still don't know about me."

Jake shook his head. "I didn't know I'd hate losing this much."

"Nobody likes losing," Quinn O'Dell said. "It's just that everybody else finds a way to get over it except you."

Quinn went and stood in the goal then, told Jake he'd give him one penalty kick for the championship of today. As Jake set the ball down, Quinn said,

"I'm gonna say this just one time and then I'm never gonna say it again: If winning is the only reason you play, then go join the Photography Club or something, because they never lose."

Jake didn't say anything to that. He just stepped back, measured his shot, decided to go high, and watched as Quinn went as high as he could, deflected the ball just enough with his left hand, and pushed it just barely over the crossbar.

Then he smiled at Jake.

"Loser," he said.

THIRTEEN

Kevin Crosby wasn't at school on Monday or Tuesday, which meant that he wasn't at practice on Tuesday, either.

So Kevin was the one guy on their team who didn't get to see the new attitude Jake brought with him to practice Tuesday night. Didn't see Jake trying to keep a smile on his face practically the whole time, even when it started to rain and he ended up doing a couple of headers into the mud.

If Quinn wanted to see fun from him, then okay, Jake was going to give him fun.

He was the one who went chasing after balls that went flying off the field and into the trees, he was the one acting like a cheerleader when he wasn't on the field for one of the three-on-two drills, he was the one patting guys on the back when they started scrimmaging and every time somebody would make a good pass or play or stop.

It was during a water break near the end of practice when Quinn came up behind him, put a hand on his shoulder, and said in a quiet voice, "Dude, you've got to dial it down a little."

Jake said, "I'm trying to set an example."

"As what, a golden retriever?"

"You told me to have fun."

"No offense, but try having a little less."

Jake kept hustling to the end, threw himself around so much that Reid McDonough—who lived to throw *himself* around—had to remind him at one point that they were playing soccer, not rugby.

When Coach finally told them he was calling it a night and that he'd see them Thursday, he jogged over to where Jake was collecting up the orange cones on the other side of the field.

"What got into *you* tonight?" Coach Lord said, and Jake said, "Just soccer."

They lost again on Saturday, to Hollis this time, 5–4.

They discovered when the game was over that

it was Hollis's first win of the season, which explained the Hollis players running around on their home field as if they'd beaten one of the teams from the English Premier League, not one even worse than theirs from Madison County, USA.

Hollis had scored its winning goal off a corner kick in the last minute, a shot that was pure luck—at least for Hollis—because Quinn seemed to have the ball all the way, even as it came down in a crowd in front of him. He went up higher than everybody else and seemed to have it until he collided with Reid.

The collision knocked the ball out of Quinn's hands and even though he tried to crawl after it on his belly, looking like a sand crab, he couldn't stop the ball from rolling over the line for the goal that beat them.

Jake had probably played his best game. It was nothing he'd ever say, not even to his parents. It was just something he knew, because you always knew in your heart how much you put into a game and how much you got back, how much you left out there. You didn't have to say it, because nobody did. It was just *in* you when you walked off the field.

And that's what it was like when Jake walked off Hollis's field.

He hadn't scored a goal, but he'd had two assists, and really had two more on top of that because of the way he'd turned the ball around and started scoring plays for Cal that had no chance of happening without him. Like he was the first domino to fall, the one that got everything going.

All this on a day when he knew he'd defended even better than he'd played on offense, breaking up plays, making slide tackles at midfield, letting Hollis know that he was going to be all over the field if that's what it took.

Even when they finally tried to shadow him with their center mid, Jake would brush the kid off like a fly and go find the ball again.

It still wasn't enough.

When the ball would get past him, down into their end, Belmont's defense in front of Quinn was sloppy. When the defenders did their job, it was Quinn who got sloppy, twice mistiming his jumps on high shots and then watching helplessly as the ball fell behind him like a home run in baseball that has just enough distance to get over the fence.

When it was over, Quinn said, "You did every-thing you could today. I was the one who let us down."

It was just the two of them walking toward the parking lot. Jake's mom and dad were going to drive them the twenty minutes or so back to Belmont.

"Shut it," Jake said.

"It's true and you know it."

"They were better," Jake said. "They made mistakes, they just made less than us, and some-times that's all it takes to know that they're better. And by the way? They wouldn't even have gotten that last corner if I hadn't gotten stripped right before it."

Jake made himself smile. "Hey, we're getting closer. We'll get 'em next week."

He didn't mean a word of that, but Quinn seemed to buy it.

FOURTEEN

Jake didn't go to the library the next day, even though he thought about it.

He knew from all the time he'd spent there how many books there were about winning. As soon as this sports star or that sports star would win a championship or have some kind of dream season, they'd write a book about it.

And there weren't just books about winning seasons, Jake knew. There were all these books by coaches, telling you how to be a winner in life. Pat Riley, the basketball coach, had a book he'd written called *The Winner Within*. Yeah, Jake was thinking now, but what the heck did you do when the winner within you couldn't get *out*?

There were all these books in the library, and not just about sports, that taught you how to get better at things, from making money to losing weight.

There had to be a book that told you how to get better at losing.

Just for fun—well, not real fun—he'd gone on the computer and typed in "Pelé's worst season." And what had come up were a lot of stories that were really about the player Ronaldo, and his Real Madrid team, and how there was a time when everybody was getting after the great striker because Real Madrid was about to go three straight seasons without winning what was known as the Champions League.

That year Pelé had said something in the newspaper about Ronaldo being "mixed up."

Ronaldo had come back at Pelé and accused him of saying "stupid things."

While reading about silly stuff like what they were saying back and forth, Jake started to think that maybe nobody really knew how to deal with losing, no matter who they were or how much money they'd made or how much winning they'd done in their lives.

So maybe, Jake thought, there weren't any

books that you could read—everybody just had to find a way to figure it out for themselves.

So he wasn't going to read anymore today.

What he needed to do was run.

Get his ball and get on his bike and ride over to school and have the soccer field there to himself. Sometimes running around didn't just make him feel better, it made him think better, too.

He didn't want to just go out in the backyard today. He didn't even want to have Quinn for company, and he didn't want his mom to come out and tell him that everything was going to work out.

Jake just needed to have open field all around him.

His parents were in the kitchen when he came down with his ball and told them where he was going. His mom asked if he wanted some company, and his dad said he'd even come along.

"Dad," Jake said, "the last time you played goal, didn't you pull something?"

His dad immediately put the newspaper up in front of his face. From behind it, Steve Stuart said, "I'm not answering that without a lawyer present."

"You *are* a lawyer."

They all laughed then. Jake thanked his parents for the offer, but said he just felt like goofing around on his own.

Jake stuffed the ball into the basket his dad had attached to the back of his bike seat and put his cleats in there with it. He rode past the corner of Kevin's block—he'd finally come back to school on Friday, but nobody knew what had been wrong with him—didn't even think about stopping at his house and asking if he wanted to come along.

Today Jake wanted to be as alone as Kevin always did.

No lousy season today, no lousy team, no bad losses. Nobody keeping score. Jake didn't have to look up at another scoreboard and see they were losing again, by a goal or two or five.

Or more.

Just him and his ball and all this green around him.

Jake ran, working up a good sweat almost right away underneath what felt like a summer sun.

Not the kind of soccer running you did to get in shape or stay in shape, not the kind Coach made you do at the end of practice, or when you messed up on something. He just ran, like if he kept running then the season couldn't catch him.

Sometimes he'd push the ball up the field, fast as he could, using only his right foot. Then he'd come back using his left. Sometimes he'd zigzag his way from one end to the other, like a broken-field runner eluding tacklers in a football game. Sometimes he'd throw the ball high up in the air ahead of him and run underneath it, like a wide receiver catching up with a long pass—only Jake wouldn't catch it with his hands, he'd try to catch it just right with his head.

And if he did *that* just right, timed it perfectly, he'd run after the ball and try to do it again.

He wasn't shooting so much today.

Just playing.

Playing to play, like Quinn had said.

He was wearing the Zidane jersey he'd bought for himself online with his birthday money, not because Zidane had head-butted the guy—the dumbest possible thing, in the biggest possible game—but because Jake had always loved the way the guy *played* the game, and hated the idea that he was

going to be remembered more for one truly amazing epic stupid play than for being the star he'd always been.

Jake looked at it this way: If Zidane could get
through that, Jake could get through a season like
this.

Unless . . .

Unless every season was going to be like this
now that he lived in Belmont, all the way through
travel and into high school.

Jake gave his head a good shake, getting that
thought out of his head, even though it had been
banging around inside there a lot lately.

Not today, he thought.

Then he was running again, this time without a
ball, just letting it rip, running at top speed, feeling
the breeze at his back, getting that downhill feeling
again.

All of a sudden a ball appeared from out of nowhere, about ten yards ahead of him, just as he
closed in on the goal. Like one of Coach Lord's
ghost players had given him a perfect set-up pass.

"Shoot it," Jake heard.

He turned and saw it was Kevin Crosby.

He had a soccer jersey of his own on, Jake saw.

"Bury it," Kevin shouted.

Jake turned back toward the ball, catching up with it in perfect stride, giving it one extra push to set it for himself like he was setting it on a tee, and drilled a sweet shot right underneath the crossbar.

When Jake turned back around, he saw that Kevin was already out at midfield and that the red jersey he was wearing was one from Manchester United. He even had white Manchester United shorts.

"You want to play?" Kevin said.

FIFTEEN

They played. And it only took about five minutes for Jake to realize he'd been right about something:

Kevin *could* play.

He could make a pass when he wanted to, could even make the kind of long pass that nobody on the Belmont 12's besides Jake could make. He even knew how to receive a pass and control the ball and get ready to do something with it all at once, which not everybody could.

Best of all, he could really shoot. He was right-footed all the way, and it took him too long to get set, but when he *did* get set, got himself into that little hop-skip motion you needed to drive the ball, he had as much leg as Jake did.

Maybe more.

They played for over an hour, made up drills

and shooting games, played until Jake was afraid Kevin was going to drop. Because even though he had game, he wasn't anywhere near being in real soccer shape, just because he hadn't run hard, *cared* enough to run hard, all season.

Jake wasn't worried about that. He knew enough about soccer to know that anybody could get in shape if they wanted to; there was no skill involved in that. But you pretty much had to be born having a leg like Kevin did.

So by then Jake couldn't help himself; he wasn't thinking of Kevin Crosby as some kind of pity project anymore, somebody he needed to help.

Jake was thinking of the team.

Thinking of him as a player.

Starting to think how Kevin could help *him*.

When they finished they rode their bikes back to Jake's house and went into his room. It was there that Kevin Crosby told Jake about his mom.

"She was my best friend," Kevin said in a quiet voice.

Jake saw him close his eyes, scrunch up his face like he was really thinking hard about something, knowing that he was trying as hard as he could not to cry.

Jake looked out the window for what felt like a long enough time, then looked back at him.

"You've got a mom like that," Kevin said when he opened his eyes.

"Yeah," Jake said. "I do."

Kevin said, "She was a writer. A good one. First for newspapers, then just once in a while for magazines after she had me. And she was writing a book, at least until she got sick. She even let me read some of it. It was about her and her dad, my grandpa, and how she was an only child, and about how she had to learn to love sports so they'd have something to talk about. And how they went to games together, and it made them love each other even more. And how now it was happening the same way for us. For my mom and me."

"Sounds awesome," Jake said.

"It was going to be."

For a second it was as if the book were sitting there between them.

Jake said, "You don't have to talk about this if you don't want to."

Kevin shook his head. "I *do* want to," he said. "With somebody other than my dad, or the lady doctor I've been going to. My dad's great and she's great. Then I saw you with your mom after the game the other day . . ." Kevin smiled, really smiled, for the first time since Jake had been around him. "And I just got it in my head that you *knew*. You know?"

"I think so," Jake said.

"My mom's why I love reading," Kevin said. "I mean, I probably would have loved it anyway. I just loved it more because of her." He cleared his throat now and said, "I used to go to the library on Sundays with her."

"Does your dad ever go with you?"

"One time," Kevin said. "The first Sunday I went back. You know. *After.* But his thing right now is that he wants me to get out and do things on my own. He doesn't come out and say it, but he doesn't want me sitting in my room and feeling sad. It's why he wouldn't let me quit soccer even though I wanted to."

"Good," Jake said. "You're too good to quit."

"I'm all right," Kevin said. "And sometimes

soccer is all right. I'll be out there running around and for a few minutes I'll trick myself into thinking stuff is the way it used to be. Only then I'll remember it's not. And it's not gonna be the same ever again. And I can't explain it, it's like all of a sudden I got punched in the gut and I can't catch my breath."

Jake said, "You're not quitting. So you know."

"Like I said, my dad won't let me."

"No," Jake said. "*I* won't let you. Dude, can't you see I need the help?"

"I don't want it like you do. I'm not sure I ever did even before my mom got sick."

"No worries," Jake said. "I can help you with that."

SIXTEEN

On Monday, for the first time, Kevin sat with Jake and Quinn on the bus. Before and after school.

He sat with them at lunch.

Same thing the next day.

Kevin still didn't say a lot. Jake would sneak a look at him sometimes when somebody, Quinn usually, would say something funny at the lunch table. And everybody would be laughing except Kevin. So there were times when it was as if he were still sitting by himself, even though he was sitting with them now.

He was trying, though. Jake could see it. It was the same at practice on Wednesday night as it had been the last few days at school. If you didn't know anything about anything, if you didn't know about his mom and didn't know he'd barely been going through the motions in soccer all season, you would have thought he was just one of the guys out there, not doing anything out of the ordinary.

But Jake knew it *was* out of the ordinary.

Because for the first time, Kevin *was* one of the guys.

One of Coach Lord's big lines was, "Guys, this is a *running* game." He'd say it when he thought they were dragging a little bit or dogging it, or when somebody would start walking after the ball when it got kicked out of bounds. If Coach spotted it, he would blow his whistle and remind them all over again that it was a running game.

Kevin was running tonight. A couple of times he was even far enough ahead of the play—and the ball—that he got whistled for being offsides.

And, best of all, he scored.

Scored right at the end of practice. Scored on Quinn after Jake had sent a pass into the right corner to Mike Clark, who had centered it like a total star.

Kevin was sitting there, middle of the field, twenty yards from the goal, nobody near him. It meant he had all the time he needed to get off his shot. He didn't worry about picking out an angle, just fired away. When he hit the ball, Jake could see it was going to come in low and to Quinn's left— close enough that Quinn would have a chance to make one of his diving stops.

Yet the ball was past him before he even got the chance to make a move on it. Kevin had caught it that cleanly. All Quinn could do was applaud and then Coach blew his whistle and said that Kevin's goal was a perfect way to end the night.

"Dude," Quinn yelled over to Kevin. "That shot was, like, *stupid* good."

"I got lucky," Kevin said, acting almost embarrassed to have scored. Or maybe just embarrassed to have drawn attention to himself by scoring.

"And there was nobody on me," he said.

"Dude," Quinn said. "I thought *I* was on you, till that sucker was past me." He shook his head. "You kicked me out like you were Jackie Chan."

Cal, who actually took karate lessons, said, "Had even more kick than Bruce Lee." Then he had to explain to everybody that Bruce Lee was like the legendary old-time dude of fancy kicking.

Then the rest of the guys were all down near the

goal, talking about their favorite martial arts movies and video games, most of which Jake had to admit he'd never heard of. But that didn't matter. He was smart enough to know the only thing that did matter was that for the first time, Kevin was the one at the center of things on this field.

SEVENTEEN

The last game of the season was against Green-ville.

The week before they had lost to Gardiner's Bay on the road, 3–2. Gardiner's Bay had only one win coming into the game, same as Belmont. It had been a good and even game all the way through. But then Gardiner's Bay had gotten a breakaway in the last minute, and Quinn didn't have a chance when one of their strikers made a perfect pass on a 2-on-1, and just like that Gardiner's Bay had their second win and Belmont was officially eliminated from the playoffs.

But this hadn't felt like the kind of loss they'd had earlier in the season. Sure, they'd lost to a team they were sure they were better than. But Belmont had played as a team against Gardiner's Bay, could see all their work starting to come together. Instead of feeling like they were expected to lose, they felt like they were one break away from getting themselves another win.

It was why, even though they only had one last regular season game to play, the kids from Belmont couldn't wait for next Saturday. Jake felt that way most of all, because the game would be against his old teammates, the Greenville Rams.

At the beginning of the season, Jake couldn't wait for the season to be over. Only now he just wanted to get right back out there. It's one of the things Jake always heard big-league baseball players talking about, how the best thing about what they did for a living was that there was a game practically every day, that you could get right back out there the next day if you lost.

That's the way Jake felt all week as he got closer to facing his friends from Greenville. And it was more than that, more than who the opponent was. Jake just wanted to finish the season on a high note, wanted to walk away from the season feeling better about himself, and his team, and the season.

And he loved the fact that Belmont had the chance to play the role of spoiler.

Greenville may have been 8-0 and in first place again. But it turned out they needed this game. Their rivals from Lincoln were 8-0-1 and had already finished their season. The game between the two of them had been called at 0–0 because of a lightning storm, and because of scheduling problems, they'd never been able to replay it. So now the top seed going into the tournament was up for grabs, which meant no ties allowed.

Playoff rules.

If Greenville won, the number one seed belonged to them. If they lost, it belonged to Lincoln. And Greenville had been the number one seed going into the tournament, Jake knew, for the last ten years.

This game mattered, big time.

Which meant it mattered to Jake just as much.

"It's almost like the playoffs are starting early," Jake said on the way to the game, sitting between Quinn and Kevin in the backseat.

Quinn said, "Dude, I hate to break this to you, but we're not going to the playoffs."

"I'm just saying," Jake said. "Who would have

thought at the beginning of the season that we'd have anything even coming close to feeling like a big game this season?"

Quinn didn't have an answer for that one. Like Jake had beaten him cleanly with a shot.

"Oh, yeah," Jake said. "I am so feeling this."

"You sure you're not just feeling the pancakes I watched you scarf for breakfast?" Quinn said.

From the front seat Jake's mom said, "Mr. O'Dell, I don't recall you complaining while you were inhaling my delicious Saturday-morning hotcakes."

"Inhaling? That is cold, Mrs. S," Quinn said. "You make me sound like some sort of vacuum cleaner."

"You just need to be a vacuum cleaner when they start firing shots at you today," Kevin said.

Jake could see his mom's reflection smiling at them from the rearview mirror. "I *thought* there was a third member of the team in the car," she said. "Not that you ever get to talk, Kevin."

"He's not a big talker, Mrs. S. But he does have the biggest leg on our team."

"Not even close," Kevin said.

"No lie," Quinn said. "He kicks so hard my foot starts to hurt just watching him."

Jake grinned. "Don't you have to take your foot out of your mouth first?"

"Look who's talking," Quinn said.

Jake saw his mom smiling again, the way she usually did listening to the conversation coming from the back of her car.

"Let's face it, Kevin," she said. "You got stuck with a bad seat."

"No," he said. "I'm good."

For once, Jake believed him.

Even without Jake—and as much as Jake hated to admit this—Greenville was better this season than last. Jake knew they had added this amazing player from Ghana, a kid named Kofi, and that he was playing center mid for the Rams now.

On the field now at Belmont Middle, Quinn was talking again as they warmed up about how he and his dad had gone to watch them beat Franklin Park 6–1, saying, "I still can't decide whether those guys remind me more of Manchester United or Arsenal."

"You sound like you don't think either Man U or Arsenal could beat them," Kevin said.

Jake said, "How about we just worry about us beating them?"

More than anything, Jake just wanted to give them a game. There was no way this would be one of Belmont's mutt-ugly losses from the beginning of the season, one of those games that seemed to be over almost as soon as it started.

One of those clock-watching games.

He wasn't going to admit this to Quinn or Kevin or his mom or Coach or anybody, but he did not want the guys on his old team, winning this season even bigger than they ever had, to come here today and look at Jake as some kind of pathetic, world-class loser.

Jake knew Belmont didn't stack up with them, knew that if this Kofi was as good as Quinn said he was and as Jake had heard he was, then there wasn't going to be a single position on the field where Belmont had an edge on them.

Not even at Jake's own position, center mid.

All week long, Jake had been thinking about one of the best things he'd ever heard anybody say about sports. It was something he'd gotten from his dad, who'd read it in a newspaper article one time. The man who'd said it was Steve Bornstein, whom his dad said used to be the boss of ESPN and was now the boss of the NFL Network.

Mr. Bornstein had been asked one time to explain why ESPN and sports just seemed to keep getting bigger and bigger. His answer was simple:

"Because you can't go to Blockbuster and rent tonight's game."

No matter what the odds said and no matter how sure people were about how a game was going to come out, it wasn't like a movie where the ending was the same every single time.

Jake wanted to believe that today, had to *make* himself believe that, as much as he ever had. Because if he didn't, he wasn't going to get anybody else on their team to believe along with him.

You can't rent today's game, he kept telling himself over and over.

Even if the game was against the Greenville Rams.

• • •

Every other team in their league showed up for road games in their parents' cars. Greenville was different, Jake knew. The Rams came in a small red bus they rented from Greenville High School.

Jake watched the bus pull up now in the parking lot closest to the field, saw Coach Ben Francis come down the steps first, then their keeper, Larry Campanelli, then Johnny Gilman, the striker who hadn't grown very much over the past year.

Then the rest of them were coming down the steps: Blake Marooney and Joe Healey, who'd played right middie on the 11's, and Paul Barberie, Jake's old wingman, the one who'd scored the goal to win last year's championship.

And in that moment Jake couldn't help it, he saw himself right there with them, in one of those white road jerseys with red trim, coming down those steps as a Greenville Ram.

Next to him Quinn said, "You look like your dog just ran away."

"You know I don't have a dog."

"In that case," Quinn said, "I didn't know how sad *that* was making you until right now."

Jake couldn't help himself. He laughed. Loudly. Quinn could almost always make him laugh and sometimes it was as if he felt it was his job as much as making saves.

Jake jogged over to say hello to his old teammates then, not waiting to see if they'd do the same. When they were around him, making fun of his Belmont uniform, Blake said, "Hey, I wondered whatever happened to you."

Larry Campanelli said, "We heard you gave up soccer for field hockey."

"Wait," Joe Healey said, "isn't field hockey a girls' sport?"

"Never mind," Larry said.

The only one who didn't come over was the new guy, Kofi. He was about thirty yards down the field from them on the sideline, doing tricks with his ball. Jake noticed he had just about the skinniest legs he'd ever seen.

Jake pointed to him and said, "Is he as good as I've heard?"

"Better," Paul Barberie said. "He doesn't just have high school coaches coming to watch him already, he's got *college* coaches."

"Of course he's not as good as the guy we used to have at center mid," Paul said. "Jake somebody."

"Very funny," Jake said.

Then Johnny Gilman said, "I hear your season has been kind of funny. Just not in a good way."

Johnny had always been Jake's least favorite kid on the team, even when they were winning games together. Johnny had thought center mid was *his* best position, even though he was the only one on the team who thought that. Jake always felt Johnny blamed him for that so he didn't have to blame Coach Francis.

"We've gotten better as the season has gone along," Jake said.

"You get points for that now in soccer?" Johnny said. "Like getting medals for trying? Wow."

Jake knew that Johnny was poking him on purpose, trying to get a reaction. He didn't think of it as being mean, and he'd been the same way when he and Jake were teammates, trash-talking him every chance he got, during practice and during games and even on the bus. But Jake wasn't going to give the guy the satisfaction of losing his temper before the game started.

So he just said to the whole group, "Have a good game."

In a scared, high-pitched voice Johnny Gilman said, "We'll . . . we'll try."

The last thing Jake heard as he ran off to join his new teammates was laughter from his old ones.

And that was all right with him. As much as Johnny Gilman could still get on his nerves—Johnny was just being Johnny—and as much as the laughter burned him, Jake was still glad he'd made the effort to go over there. Because even though he didn't know how the game was going to come out, he knew this:

He wasn't with those guys anymore.

EIGHTEEN

Paul Barberie scored the first goal of the game, off a sweet pass from Kofi.

Who Jake could already see was everything he'd heard.

Everything and more.

It happened five minutes into the game. Kofi lost Jake the way you lose socks, faked out Reid so badly that Reid fell down. Finally he Zidaned a pass behind his back to Paul, who drilled a low hard shot to Quinn's right. Paul was the same kind of finisher he'd been when Jake was the one passing him the ball.

Jake nearly ran over to Paul, by force of habit, and high-fived him.

But he didn't.

Instead he brought Belmont right back.

Two minutes later, Kofi tried another one of his fancy stops at midfield, the kind of twirl you only saw from figure skaters at the Olympics. Only this time it was as if he'd faked himself out, and he fell down.

As soon as he did, Jake was on him, taking the ball from him, up and running at full speed right away. He had Kevin and Cal as wingmen and their striker, Tim Fox, so far on the outside the Greenville fullbacks weren't even paying attention to him.

They weren't watching Kevin very much, either.

All eyes were on a former Greenville Ram.

Jake.

Jake felt it, *saw* them focused on him, saw the whole field—at least the part that mattered now, which meant the box in front of him. He didn't turn around, no time for that, knowing Kofi had to be chasing the play on those skinny legs of his, coming hard because that's what Jake would have done if he'd just made the kind of bad turnover Kofi had.

Jake knew they'd be expecting him to pass, even in as deep as he was, just because they knew him so well. Blake, their stopper, had to be thinking that way and so did Larry Campanelli, who was scoping everything out from in front of the goal.

Blake decided to force the play. But as soon as he moved up, Jake ducked his shoulder, pushed the ball behind him with his right leg, and picked it up with his left. It was the same as him waving goodbye.

Jake watched Larry Campanelli's eyes now, locked on Larry, saw those eyes leave him for just a second, because here came Tim Fox from Larry's left.

Thank you, Jake thought.

He didn't wait now. And he sure didn't pass. Instead, he blasted away with the hardest shot he'd taken all year. Quinn would joke later that even at the other end of the field, the shot sounded like a tire exploding.

Jake knew Larry was better going to his right, so he put it high and hard over his left shoulder, into the corner.

Just like that, it was 1–1.

It was just one goal. It was still early. Greenville was still Greenville, Jake knew that as well as anybody on the field. But the player in him, all the jock in him, knew something else. Just knew.

It was game on now.

Oh, yeah.

It was *on*.

Kofi scored not long after to make it 2–1 for Greenville, smoked one left-footed from just outside the box, as if he somehow needed to get off an even better shot than Jake had.

The goal came with 4:30 left in the half, and Kofi should have gotten another one about a minute later. But he waited too long after getting behind everybody, and Quinn flashed out and threw himself on the ball just as Kofi was about to drive his leg through.

Save of the game.

At least it was until Quinn made an even better one with under a minute left.

On that one, Kofi pulled him out of position before pushing a pass over to Johnny Gilman, who seemed to have the entire goal wide open to him, like an open door. It made him too careful. Instead of blasting away, he just pushed the ball toward the net and somehow Quinn got back into the play, dove to his left, caught the ball, jumped up and booted the ball down the field.

To Jake.

He caught the ball off his chest, controlled it, sent it ahead to Cal, who passed it to Tim, streaking in again from the right.

Larry Campanelli had no chance.

It was still 2–2 when the whistle blew ending the half.

The longer Belmont stayed in the game, the more frustrated Jake's old teammates became.

And the more they started to act less and less like Jake's old friends.

Johnny Gilman tried to get into Jake's ear, and maybe in his head, talking even more smack in the second half than he had in the first. Then it was more than talk, Johnny tripping Jake as he was carrying the ball out of his own end, getting whistled for a penalty in the process.

Now Johnny wasn't the only one doing the talking. It was Paul Barberie, too, waiting until the ref was out of earshot before saying to Jake, "Nice flop."

"You're kidding, right?" Jake said. "Guy tripped me from behind."

Paul shook his head. "You never begged for calls when you played for us."

Jake said, "Well, I don't play for you anymore," and walked away from him.

After all the great scoring chances in the first half, more Greenville than Belmont, more Kofi than anybody else on the field, the second half was more about defense and the keepers, with Quinn and Larry Campanelli making it look easy the few times they were asked to make saves.

The game stayed 2–2 but somehow kept getting better, the way soccer could even when nobody was able to get the ball into the goal, when there was so much good action, so much offense and defense and so many great saves, you forgot that nobody was actually scoring.

Everything Quinn had said about playing just to play, everything Jake had said to Kevin about that, it was all on the field now. All *over* the field.

Belmont's 12's weren't doing this against Gardiner's Bay now. They were doing it against *Greenville,* the best team in their league and maybe the best team of 12's in the whole state.

During a stop in play with ten minutes left, Jake gathered his teammates around him and pointed out at Kofi, dancing on his toes at midfield, as if he couldn't wait for the timeout to be over so he could start running again and get after Belmont all over again.

"That guy is a better player than I ever thought of being," Jake said.

It was Kevin who said, "No way."

It was the first thing he'd said in a huddle like this all season.

"Way," Jake said. "But I want you guys all to know I'm not gonna let him be better today. I'm not gonna let him beat us. I'm gonna try to beat him on every ball and I want everybody on this team to do the same with their man."

He looked around. "That means we all man up like we never have in our lives," he said.

Jake put his hand out now. His teammates leaned in, put theirs on top of it.

"*Man up!*" they yelled, in one voice.

With four minutes left, Kofi set up Johnny Gilman beautifully. But Johnny, trying to make up for the kick he'd babied earlier, kicked this one wild and high, slapping his thigh in frustration afterward.

Our turn, Jake thought.

But their turn didn't come until there was less than a half-minute left, the game still tied 2–2.

Kofi had the ball for Greenville, trying to find an opening for himself. He sent a long pass toward Johnny Gilman. But Jake saw it coming, read it the whole way, picked it off at midfield, and controlled it like a dream.

He began taking it the other way.

Cal was somewhere out to his left. Kevin was running alongside Jake on his right. And because the play had turned around so quickly, the way soccer could—the sudden U-turns being one of the things Jake loved most about the sport—the Greenville defenders were slow to react.

Slow to react with Jake and Cal and Kevin coming at them fast.

Jake gave one quick thought to firing the ball

at Larry Campanelli himself, trying his first left-footed shot of the day, because that was the best angle he had.

Only it wasn't the right play, and Jake always wanted to make the right play, first minute of the game or the last, first game of the season or the last, even if the last game was against his former teammates on the Greenville Rams.

So he swung his left foot in front of him and passed the ball to Kevin, seeing what was going to happen inside his head before it happened, knew in that moment that this wasn't going to be just his day and Belmont's day.

It was going to be Kevin's day, too.

He would be the one to beat Greenville.

The pass could only be described by one of Quinn's favorite words.

It was *dirty*.

Right before the ball got to Kevin, Jake whipped his head around, saw the clock showing ten seconds left.

All day, even for Kevin.

Let it rip, Jake thought.

Kevin did.

His angle, his opening, was to Larry's right, and that's where he went with the ball. And as good as Larry had been all day, he was just a beat slow now.

Or maybe he just didn't know how much leg Kevin had.

Jake was the one with the best angle on the play now, a great look at the ball as Kevin caught it just right, as cleanly as he ever could, with all the leg he had, and smoked it toward the far corner.

Goal! Jake thought.

He was wrong.

The hook Kevin had put on the ball made it clip the outside of the post and bounce all the way off the field with the score still 2–2.

The whistle blew, three times.

End of regulation.

No ties allowed. No overtime.

Shoot-out.

NINETEEN

Jake allowed himself about one minute to feel defeated, feel as if they'd lost the game even though there was still more game to be played.

Allowed himself one minute to stand there, frozen, to Larry Campanelli's right and feel as if their best chance to upset Greenville had just come and gone, that maybe Kevin had wanted the game too much the way they all wanted it too much. That's why he'd put too much into what would have been the greatest shot of his life.

That was *our* shot, Jake thought. Only the Rams had taken it.

Jake may have felt like he no longer knew his former teammates on Greenville, but as he stood there in the middle of the field, he did know this:

The Rams had more firepower than Belmont,

and that was about to come into play in the shoot-out.

Big time.

Jake knew how many shooters the Rams had because he had been one of those shooters once.

But then he knew something more important, that he had to stop feeling sorry for himself. Right now. Because if you were really a team leader, you weren't allowed to do that. You didn't point fingers, didn't hang your head. If you got knocked down, you picked yourself back up. That was the deal.

Jake's team needed him. And so did Kevin Crosby. Maybe now more than ever. Kevin was standing in the same spot where he'd taken his shot, looking as if he was the one who wanted to run somewhere and hide, looking as sad as he ever had, like he'd turned back into the kid who didn't want to be here.

Jake ran for him, knowing how much he needed to tell Kevin before the shoot-out started. Knowing how little time he had.

Like he had to beat the clock all over again.

"Listen to me," Jake said.

"No," Kevin said, still staring off in the direction

where his shot had run away from Larry and every-body else.

Jake put his hands on Kevin's shoulder, the way Coach did sometimes, knowing this was the most important coaching he was ever going to do on the field, and said, "Yes."

Kevin looked at him, even though Jake knew he didn't want to.

"The shot should've gone," Jake said. "And you know that."

"But it didn't."

"It was a *killer* shot," Jake said. "It was just like a line drive that hooked foul at the very end."

"Except this foul ball counted as strike three," Kevin said.

Over Kevin's shoulder, Jake could see Coach Lord waving him over to the sidelines.

Jake put up a finger.

This was more important.

"Think of all the times when nobody on this team had a shot like that against a team like this," Jake said. "But you had the shot, don't you get it? And I know you feel like we just lost, but we didn't lose."

"I'm tired of people telling me stuff is all right when it's not," Kevin said.

"Jake!"

Coach Lord.

Halfway out on the field now.

"You're missing the point," Jake said.

"Yeah, like I missed the net."

"We're a real team now," Jake said. "And there's nothing better than that. It took me a long time to get it. But now I do. We're a team and we've gone toe-to-toe with the best stinking team in our league, and now we've still got a chance to clip them in a shoot-out, beat them out of a game they thought they couldn't lose on a bet. That's what this is all about, the feeling that we've had all day—the one we're gonna get back as soon as we get over to Coach before he grounds me for life."

Kevin still didn't look as if he was buying what Jake was trying to sell.

"What feeling is that?" Kevin said.

Jake grinned. "The feeling that you get from sports when you think you've given everything you've got . . . and then you find out you've got even more."

• • •

"Listen," Coach Lord said when they got over to him. "This is no time for a long speech. I just want to say that you guys played your hearts out today, like no team I've ever had, and that's all any coach could ask for."

He was turning to his left and right, as if trying to look into the face of everybody on the team.

He said, "I'm not going to say that you guys made me proud today, because that's never what this is about. You did something much better than that, the only thing that ever really matters: You made yourselves proud."

Nobody said anything. The only thing you could hear in the huddle was players breathing.

The ones who *were* breathing, anyway.

"And nothing is going to happen over the next few minutes that's going to change that," Coach finished.

Then he gave them the order for their five shooters in the shoot-out:

Cal Morris.

Tim Fox.

Reid McDonough.

Mike Clark.

Jake.

The kick he'd dreamed about taking his whole life.

It wasn't the World Cup. It wasn't the league championship or even an official playoff game.

It just felt like all that.

Felt like that because they had become a team, had become more than they were supposed to be, and had played a game like this against the Rams.

Yeah, Jake thought.

Today was the championship of all that.

Greenville had the first shot. The ball was placed on its mark, middle of the field, twelve yards from the chalk line in front of their goal.

Jake hadn't said anything to Quinn when it was time for him to run out and take his place in front of the goal, because there was nothing left for anybody to say. The time for talking was over.

Jake just looked at him, put out his fist, and gave him some pound.

Then they both twisted their wrists, locking it up the way they did.

Blake Marooney was first up for Greenville.

He didn't waste any time, blasting one with his huge left foot over Quinn's left shoulder.

Just like that, it was 1–0, Greenville.

Belmont's turn.

Larry Campanelli guessed right on Cal's shot, diving to his right as Cal let the ball go, catching it cleanly.

Still Greenville, 1–0.

Jake was always amazed, watching shoot-outs on television, how after a long game, everything was suddenly happening in fast-forward, how you felt as if you didn't have a chance to catch your breath between kicks.

Paul Barberie tried to go low to Quinn's right, but shot it wide, hooked it the way Kevin had earlier.

Still 1–0.

Quinn jumped up, looking like he wanted to celebrate, just because it hadn't gone to 2–0, but Jake could see him pulling himself back. Instead he looked over at Jake, made a small fist, locked it up in the air in front of him.

Jake did the same.

Tim Fox next for Belmont. Jake knew what a good player Tim was, knew how accurate a kicker he could be, knew what good decisions he always made on the field. But he also knew that Tim didn't have the strongest leg on the team.

No worries.

He was a right-footed kicker and Larry Campanelli knew that. But Tim crossed him up, crossed everyone up, by going with his left.

Went high to the corner to Larry's left.

Nothing but net.

1–1.

Quinn then stopped Joe Healey, diving neatly to his left and knocking away a sharp line drive. There was this huge cheer now from the Belmont stands, the moms and dads and everybody else in the bleachers sounding to Jake like one of those soccer stadiums in Europe during the Euro playoff games he'd watched on television.

Still 1–1.

Reid's turn. He made solid contact, and seemed to have controlled his own big leg for once. But Larry somehow made a stop that looked like a special effect from the movies, catching the ball in his gloves even after it was behind him.

Jake was pacing now, moving up and down the sidelines, not wanting to ice himself the way basketball teams iced shooters.

Knowing his moment was coming.

He stopped to watch Quinn make a stop on Johnny Gilman, Jake wanting to cheer as he did. Johnny wasn't doing any talking now, didn't have any mouth on him, just running past the Belmont bench with his head down.

Mike Clark now.

Mike stumbled slightly as he moved into his kick, as if he was unsure where to send the ball, and that little bit of hesitation seemed to throw Larry off. What should have been an easy shot for him to block, not much on it, instead bounced over his outstretched hands and into the goal.

2–1, Belmont.

Wow, thought Jake.

Wow.

If Quinn stopped Kofi, it was over.

And if Kofi scored, it would come down to Jake.

Jake almost didn't know which way to root.

He didn't have long to think about it. Kofi made the decision for him, with his own spin on the old Beckham bend, hitting a shot that seemed to be going for the middle of Quinn's chest until it broke away from him like a late-breaking fastball, and into the far corner as Quinn ended up face-first in the dirt in front of the goal, pounding both fists into the ground in frustration.

He came over to the sidelines now, dirt on both his cheeks, looking like he wanted to punch something much harder than the ground.

"Tell me you got this," he said to Jake. "Please tell me you got this."

"I got this," Jake said.

"You know what you're going to do?"

Jake turned around then.

Looked into the crowd, at his mom and dad. Looked down the sidelines at his teammates. Saw Kevin, still looking as though he'd let everyone down.

Jake turned back to Quinn, his best bud in the world, and smiled.

"Yeah, I know exactly what I'm going to do," he said.

He set the ball down on the mark one last time. The same mark Jake had painted into his back lawn, in front of his goal.

Where he'd been practicing for this shot his whole life.

Coach Lord said, "Okay, Jake. Go win us the game."

"No," Jake said.

"Very funny," Coach Lord said. "I'm always for lightening the mood. Now get out there."

Jake smiled at him, as if he and Coach were the only ones in on the joke.

Except it was no joke.

"We're winning the game, Coach. You got that part right," Jake said. "But I'm not taking the last kick."

He turned to Kevin Crosby.

"You are," Jake said.

TWENTY

Coach Lord stared at Jake, no expression. Blank wall.

Then he smiled back at him.

As if somehow he knew that even though it wasn't going to be Jake's shot, this was his call, that in the biggest moment of the season—a moment that felt like their whole season—Jake was doing exactly what Coach Lord had asked him to do with Kevin Crosby, way back at the beginning.

Kevin hadn't moved, but was shaking his head now, saying, "Coach, Jake should take the shot. He's our best player."

Coach said, "You may be right about that, Kevin. But you're our best leg."

The ref was a few yards away, blowing his whistle again, looking annoyed, yelling that if they didn't get back out there and take the shot, there wouldn't be one.

Kevin said, "I just used that leg to kick one toward Elm Street."

"So this time you're going to kick a hole in their net," Jake said. "We need you, Kevin."

The rest of the Belmont players had been listening in silence. Now Quinn, as usual, broke the silence.

"Ke-vin, Ke-vin, Ke-vin," he began chanting, and then the rest of the team joined in. "Ke-vin, Ke-vin, KE-VIN."

Kevin was still shaking his head, but now he came to stand next to Jake. "You're sure you want to do this?" he asked.

"Center mids are supposed to set up the best shot," Jake answered. "And you're ours."

Then Jake quietly told Kevin he'd been watching Larry Campanelli's moves in goal practically his whole life, and told him exactly where to shoot it. Then he took his place outside the box with the rest of the players on both teams.

The only two players inside the box were Kevin and Larry, shooter and keeper.

Jake was surprised at how quiet it got then, even with big crowds on both sides of the field. Almost library-quiet as Kevin took his place behind the ball.

Jake looked over again to where he knew his mom and dad were sitting on the Belmont side, saw his mom looking right at him, as if she'd been waiting for him to look at her.

She pounded her chest twice, just the way he'd showed her.

He wondered if Kevin was thinking about his mom.

Wait, Jake had told Kevin.

Wait just one split-second before you swing that leg of yours. Fake your approach. Jake was sure Larry would flash to his right the way he had plenty of times before, make the percentage move for most right-footed kickers, especially right-footed kickers their age, most of whom just blasted away.

The ref blew the whistle for the last time that day.

Kevin made his hop-step into the ball.

Larry threw himself to his right.

As soon as he did, Kevin Crosby kicked with

everything he had. Only this time, he knew exactly where the ball was headed. He placed it right on the empty spot Larry had just left wide open.

Dead center on goal.

Hit it so hard and clean Jake really did think it was going to put a hole in the net.

Belmont 3, Greenville 2.

When Kevin finally broke loose from the rest of their teammates, he got up from the bottom of the pile of Belmont players and hugged his dad. Jake walked over to them.

Before he could say anything, Kevin did.

"Thank you," he said.

"Dude," Jake said. "You just beat my old team for me. Are you insane? Thank *you*."

Kevin looked around now, as if taking a snapshot of the scene around him, the whole day.

"So this is what it feels like," he said.

"Making a kick like that?" Jake said.

"Being happy," Kevin said.

Now Jake was the one looking around, taking it all in, soccer looking as perfect to him as it ever had, the way a good center mid wanted it to look:

Everybody exactly where they were supposed to be.

"Yeah," he said, and felt himself smile, at Kevin, at the day. "This is what it feels like."

ABOUT THE AUTHOR

Mike Lupica, over the span of his successful career as a sports columnist, has proven that he can write for sports fans of all ages and stripes. And as the author of multiple hit books for young readers, including *Heat, Travel Team, The Big Field, Million-Dollar Throw,* and *The Batboy,* among others, Mr. Lupica has carved out a niche as the sporting world's finest storyteller.

Mr. Lupica, whose column for New York's *Daily News* is syndicated nationally, lives in Connecticut with his wife and their four children. He can be seen weekly on ESPN's *The Sports Reporters.*